RESCUING SINGLE MOM

TURNING GOOD BOOK 1

SUZANNE HART

© **Copyright 2019 by Suzanne Hart - All rights reserved.**

In no way is it legal to reproduce, duplicate, or transmit any part of this document in either electronic means or in printed format. Recording of this publication is strictly prohibited and any storage of this document is not allowed unless with written permission from the publisher. All rights reserved.

Respective authors own all copyrights not held by the publisher.

WARNING: This eBook contains sexually explicit scenes and adult language. It may be considered offensive to some readers. This eBook is for sale to adults ONLY.

Please ensure this eBook is stored somewhere that cannot be accessed by underage readers.

CONTENTS

1. Silas	1
2. Iris	6
3. Silas	11
4. Iris	16
5. Silas	21
6. Iris	26
7. Silas	31
8. Iris	35
9. Silas	43
10. Iris	47
11. Silas	51
12. Iris	55
13. Silas	59
14. Iris	63
15. Silas	67
16. Iris	71
17. Silas	75
18. Iris	79
19. Silas	87
20. Iris	91
21. Silas	95
22. Iris	99
23. Silas	103
24. Iris	107
25. Silas	114
26. Iris	118
27. Silas	125
28. Iris	129
29. Silas	134
30. Iris	138
31. Silas	142
32. Iris	146

33. Silas	150
34. Iris	155
35. Silas	164
36. Iris	168
37. Silas	172
38. Iris	176
39. Silas	180
40. Iris	184
41. Silas	188
42. Iris	192
43. Silas	196
44. Iris	201
45. Silas	205
46. Iris	209
47. Silas	213
48. Iris	217
49. Silas	221
50. Iris	225
51. Silas	229
52. Iris	233
53. Silas	237
54. Iris	241
55. Silas	245
56. Iris	249
57. Iris	253
Bonus Epilogue	259
A note from the author	261
Also by Suzanne Hart	263

1
SILAS

We shook hands on the new deal, a twinkle radiating in my father's eyes. He was satisfied, which meant I was more than ecstatic. With Dad happy, our vision for the future was going to become more than just that, it was going to become a reality.

Before I knew it, we would be looking at a new complex of luxury apartments in the heart of the city. It was the most sought after location in Chicago. We'd won the bid against the competing real estate companies and were chomping at the bit to break ground. Our plan was ambitious, pushing to start in just four months' time, but when we were finished, the most luxurious apartments in the city would graze the skyline.

And this project was going to have the Denton name splashed all over it.

My father was a good man. He had kept his priorities straight no matter the cost, and it paid off for him in the end. Above all else, what mattered to Dad most was family, and the legacy he was eventually going to leave behind. That piece of real estate wasn't something the city was going to forget easily. We aimed for architectural perfection and interior detail that would be sought after for decades.

We stepped out of the boardroom and walked the group to the elevators. They were buzzing, voices low and teaming with excitement. Millions of dollars had just changed hands amongst us; everyone was taking a risk, but it was a risk I was sure would end in success.

When the elevator doors pinged shut, Dad turned to me with his striking ice blue eyes. His silver hair was brushed back and shimmered lightly beneath the fluorescent lights. He had one hand thrust deep in the pocket of his pinstriped three-piece suit.

I could still remember the day he had turned to me with his brows crossed and his voice strained with anger and disgust.

"You expect me to put on a suit every day and take the elevator up to an office with a fucking view? Is that what you want us to become? A couple of corporate morons?" he'd growled.

And now look at him. He was a natural, as if he had been there since day one.

"You've gone above and beyond this time, son," he said, reaching over and patting my back with pride.

I grinned at him. It didn't matter that I was thirty-five-year's old, I still thrived off of my dad's praise.

"Four months and we can begin construction," I replied as we walked toward his office.

Dad nodded, both his hands deep in his pockets now. "I trust you, Silas. You'll get this started on time."

As we approached his door, we stopped and he gripped my hand, giving it a stern shake. I smiled and watched as he headed inside, giving me a nod before closing the door behind him. My father was a pro at negotiations, doing his part to help the company thrive and succeed, but once the clients were gone, he retreated into his shell, shutting out the world.

He would never forgive himself for the past, for the fact that my brothers weren't a part of the company. He blamed himself for everything that had happened, and no amount of success, no amount of coaching could change those feelings.

With a slight shrug, I turned and walked slowly down the hall back toward my own office with a view. The sparks of excitement were still churning in my veins. I lived for those moments. But the road ahead was going to paved in hard work, long hours, and a lot of stress. Just minutes after the meeting I was facing piles of paperwork, meetings, and project proposals. As I turned the corner, my assistant, Lena came rushing toward me. She always had a panicked expression on her face, so there was no way for me to know from a distance if this was an emergency or not.

"Mr. Denton!" she exclaimed as she stopped in front of me, out of breath.

I arched my brows quizzically at her. It better be good.

"Ms. Sadie is on line One. She said she's calling from an airport and doesn't have much time."

It *was* good!

I rushed to my office, leaving Lena, hands on her knees, recovering her breath in the hallway. Without skipping a beat, I hopped over the box of files Lena had been working on transferring to the server, and swung my door shut behind me. As I slid into my leather rolling chair, I reached over and clicked the flashing button on the phone, smiling as I put the receiver to my ear.

"Well, look who has decided to surface," I said cheerfully.

My sister's voice was cheerful and light. "Hey there big brother."

"Where have you been?" I asked, almost excited to hear about her latest travels.

"Mauritius, Thailand, Bali...I'm pretty sure I went somewhere else too but it's all a haze," Sadie replied with a laugh.

I hadn't heard from her in over a month, and had finally reached a point where I stopped worrying. She was young, she had no real responsibilities, and she knew how to look after herself.

What was I doing in my early twenties?

"Sounds like fun. Are you on your way home?" I asked.

"Maybe, maybe not. I haven't decided. It's not like I'll have much to do if I come home. At least this way, I get to see the world."

She had a point.

"How is Dad?" Sadie asked.

At least she still asked about him. "He's good, the same as always, keeping busy with work. You know the drill."

"Have you heard anything from Miles lately?" Her voice was hopeful.

"Not a peep," I replied, hating to disappoint her.

She knew the next question was pointless to ask, but it had become habit. "Is Alex keeping his head above water?"

"I can't tell him what to do," I replied, shaking my head at the sound of her sigh..

Our brothers, Alex and Miles, weren't people that could be controlled or even talked to really. I was the oldest of all the kids, but I wasn't their keeper, and couldn't be even if I wanted to. They were grown men with hard head, no one could tell them what to do. They wanted to stay away, lead their own lives away from the rest of the family—especially Dad, and that was their choice.

"It was good to hear your voice, Silas, but I have to go now," Sadie said, a tinge of sadness in her voice. "My flight's boarding."

"You still don't have a cellphone? It would be good to stay in touch, Sades." I shook my head at her brilliant laughter.

"What'd be the point of trying to disconnect if I'm carrying a cellphone around?" she asked. "Don't worry about me, big brother, I'll be back soon."

With that, the line went dead and I put the receiver down on the hook with a sigh. Turning my head up toward the ceiling, I could feel that familiar frustration creeping back in. I loved my sister, and I wanted her to lead her own life, but I felt like everything was falling on my shoulders. I had always been the only one making an attempt to keep the family somewhat glued together, but day by day that glue dried up and chipped away. One day I feared, it would just be me.

2

IRIS

My eyes fluttered open slowly, focusing in on the clock by my bed. I didn't move, tucked warmly under my covers, watching the seconds tick by. It was just a few moments before my dreaded alarm would ring out, piercing my beautiful, restful sleep. I was going to be prepared this time. I was going to get out of bed with a positive mindset.

Or not...

The numbers changed and the horn blared loudly from the back of the clock's speakers. I reached for it, banging it shut, cursing it under my breath. Just like every other day of my life I crawled out of the bed with aching in my limbs and feeling as if I hadn't even begun to recover the long days before. It felt like I could lie in bed all day and I'd still be exhausted.

Unfortunately, my life was not graced with the luxury of lazing around in my pajamas, sleeping until my body actually felt rested. I never complained though, not unless it was seconds after the alarms, that was my safe time to get it out of my system. I couldn't remember the last time I had spent an extra fifteen minutes in bed.

Not since Bess came into my life.

I yawned and stretched my arms wide as I swung my legs off the edge of the bed, scrunching my toes into the shag carpet rug next to the bed. Glancing out the window I could see the few leaves from the sidewalk streets blow by. It was the middle of fall, which meant I was going to have to make sure Bess was carefully bundled up. She despised warm clothing for some reason. She liked to be free and wild. But then again, what six-year-old didn't?

I drug myself up to the small oval mirror in my bedroom and pushed the scarves and necklaces out of the way so I could take a quick look at myself. My face looked tired, my skin dry, dark circles hugging my eyes, and my hair had lost that luster and shine it had when I could spend a hundred dollars at the salon every month.

I hadn't felt attractive in months, but at the same time, it had also been months since I gave my appearance a second thought. There were far more important things to think about now, and I was okay with that... most days..

Running a quick hand through my hair, I walked out of the bedroom, finding my six-year-old, bright eyed girl sitting at the table, eating her cereal with a spoon that looked far too big for her tiny hands.

Bess was amazing. She was alarmingly helpful and intelligent for six years old, and just when I thought she was just a normal little girl she would offer some prophetic introspect into the human species. Without realizing it, I had groomed Bess to be very self-sufficient. As a single mother, it was key to our survival.

"Good morning sweetie," I said walking up behind her and lovingly squeezing her cheeks.

She had the TV on and was watching cartoons while she ate, her little legs swinging back and forth. I hadn't had to wake her up or make her breakfast in a long time, she did it all herself.

I leaned over and kissed the top of her head and she tilted back smiling at me. "Morning Mommy."

I poured myself a mug of coffee and brought it to the table, sitting down in front of her. I blocked the television, but she was used to it. We had our routine. She could watch cartoons until I came out and then it was, what she liked to call, human to human time.

I took a sip of my coffee and smiled. "How's school going, honey?"

Nothing in the world was more important to me than my daughter, and watching her blossom into a mature young girl felt like a privilege. If there was one thing I had done right, it was Bess, even though it didn't always feel like it.

"I like it, Mommy. And my new friend Amy is really nice," she said.

I watched her talk excitedly about school, leaning my chin on my palm, my heart melting all over again. It was a daily occurrence. I loved to see her happy and well adjusted. I did my best to give her a good education, a good life, and at the same time, do the kind of work that she could be proud of me for. It wasn't always easy juggling all the single mom responsibilities, but as long as my daughter was turning out okay, none of the other stuff really mattered.

After breakfast, we got ready to leave for the day. Our morning routine was getting easier as the time passed. I walked Bess to school, dropping her off with her kindergarten teacher, and then headed over to the café I managed. It was a short train ride through the city, and I didn't mind the few minutes of quiet alone time, or as alone as a city transit train could get.

Brews and Bagels was a popular midtown Chicago café that I worked at ever since I dropped out of college. I started out as a waitress but thankfully rose up to managerial status not too long after I had Bess. Managing staff wasn't easy business, but I couldn't stand the thought of flirting and making small-talk with uninteresting men just for a tip.

My manager's salary wasn't great, but it got us through the month comfortably enough. Working at a cafe that closed early also had its advantages. I was able to be there to get Bess from school most days, or at least keep her from spending long hours in daycare, and it gave me time to dedicate myself to the foundation I had started. The foundation that was second in line after Bess for my heart and soul.

The foundation was an anti-drug, non-profit agency that I had started in Chicago's Southside, close to where we lived. It blossomed about two years before, catching fire from a simple idea, with no backing, barely any funding, and no clout behind it. I believed it in though, so I pushed, learned how to do everything myself, cut corners where I could, and tried to always keep the faith. Eventually, with the help of some donations and generous volunteers, we were able to rent a hall, have a couple of low key fundraisers, and get some legs beneath the concept. With a little stability I wanted to keep that forward momentum, so I had been working diligently on building a more permanent place to do our work.

My goal was, by the end of year, I'd be able to acquire a small building where we could have a dedicated dorm room for women who were detoxing and cleaning up their lives. The organization would provide the women a safe haven, a place to get away from the drugs, abusers, and users that were toxic to their recovery. I wanted to provide those unable to afford rehab, unable to get into the clinics, a place they could go to jumpstart their recovery efforts. There were so many people that wanted the help, but gave up when the system was full.

We were already doing good work, but we could do so much more if we has more financial backers and a place to call home. It was my primary concern after me and Bess, and I was constantly working on it, even when I was at the café. In the back of mind, I was creating plans, laying out programs, and rolling over the speed bumps in the road. I was passionate about it, and that drove me every day.

There was nothing I could do to change my own past, what was done was done. But I knew that learning from that and taking active steps to help others would keep me and Bess from ever finding ourselves in a bad situation again. Two years before, at just twenty-six, stumbling through life with Bess on my hip, I didn't think the organization would actually ever go anywhere, but day by day I saw it evolving. It was beautiful.

It was Bess and the agency that kept me going, kept getting me out of bed every day, and made me believe there was still something beautiful and worth living for in the world.

I walked Bess to her school that morning, standing and watching as she waved at me, running full speed in to the school. Her smile and laughter let me know that we were going to be okay.

3

SILAS

Working late had become a normal occurrence for me. By the time I got home, it was past nine. My penthouse condo wasn't too far from the office, though, and my driver dropped me at the front. I looked up at the thirteen story apartment complex and smiled, remembering when we had finished building it. The Parks was the company's first building project, and was special to me. That was why I chose there to live, even though I could have afforded any of the luxury places through the city.

My place was the top floor, the penthouse. It was definitely the kind of condo that was highly sought after in the packed Chicago hustle and bustle, but I wasn't planning on moving anytime soon. It had three enormous bedrooms, a living room with glass front walls that looked out over the twinkling bridge lights and building jutting up toward the sky. A custom kitchen, stone accented bathrooms, and impeccable interior design made the place a sanctuary for me every time I left the office.

It was the kind of place my brother Alex would have appreciated, but would never have bought because our company owned it. He was stubborn, but that was an attribute that seemed to run in the family.

I'd been living there for close to three years and, though quiet and relaxing, it had yet to start feeling like home. Something was missing and I couldn't put my finger on it. Whatever it was, at least I had safety, shelter, and an amazing view.

I took the elevator up to my apartment, finding Carla standing in the hallway as the doors slid open. My eyes shut for a moment, not completely surprised, but definitely annoyed that she was there. I thought about pressing the button and heading back down to the lobby, but running was apparently not going to shake me of the woman.

As I exited the elevator, she stood up straight, slipping her phone into her purse and smiling as if I were supposed to be ecstatic, she was yet again at my condo without an invite. I walked right past her without a word, taking out the key to my place and swiping it through the lock.

When she talked, the hair stood up on the back of my neck. "I've been waiting close to an hour for you. I was trying to surprise you, and figured you wouldn't be just now coming in."

I didn't say a word, just opened up the door and walked inside. Of course, she followed right behind me, uninvited. I would have turned and told her to leave, but I decided I needed to end things that night because it was getting completely out of hand.

She shut the door behind us and the lights in the apartment automatically dimmed up from their lowest setting. I walked silently down the hall toward my den. I hadn't replied to her yet, but she didn't seem to notice. She trailed along behind me completely oblivious to my lack of attention. It was beyond annoying.

"You work too hard, Silas, you should seriously consider taking a break," she squawked.

I walked straight to the bar and poured myself a few fingers of Glenfiddich in a crystal glass. I didn't offer her any, and not because I knew she didn't enjoy Scotch.

"I had an uncle, uncle Matty, he worked so hard he got hemorrhoids," she continued "I'm not making this up. Stress and work pressure can do obscene things to your body."

At first glance, she was glamorous, a classic beauty. That head of beautiful bright blond hair was what made my cock throb when I first laid eyes on her at a cocktail party a month before. The host introduced us and I didn't fight it. Anything to get closer to that delicious body of hers wrapped perfectly in a tight velvet dress.

But once I'd taken that dress off in my room that night and made her mine, my interest quickly diminished. Her hair didn't quite shine in the same way in the morning light, her blue eyes looked dull and uninteresting, her shrill voice annoyed me with every tone, and I wanted her gone.

Carla could never take a hint. One month later and she was still talking non-stop, still showing up out of the blue, and still ignoring every attempt I made at shutting her down. It was obvious at that point, I was just going to have to be blunt, even if I hated being an asshole.

"And my daddy always said that a long weekend is always going to be way more precious than a business meeting ever will be," she continued.

I could feel myself coming unglued. I just wanted to be alone, enjoy my drink, and go to sleep by myself.

She'd already made herself comfortable on my couch, crossing her long shapely legs, her dress riding up her thighs. It was the sort of thing that would have normally changed my tone. That night, though, after a surprise visit and the mention of hemorrhoids, I was over it. We'd slept together four time that month already, which was four times too many. She bored me, and her incessant nagging was plucking my last nerve.

"We should go out to the islands next month," she said, looking at her nails. "We could invite another couple, make it a thing."

"You've gotta go," I growled, walking over to the den door.

Those were my first words to her that night and from the look on her face, they took her by surprise. Hadn't she been rejected by a man before?

Carla crossed her brows and stared up at me, hoping she'd heard me wrong. "Silas..."

She was starting to say something but I cut her short. "And you can't turn up here at my place unannounced anymore. It's a violation of my privacy. I told you before, I come home to be in a quiet place, and if I want you here, I'll send for you."

I wasn't about to look away from her. I wanted her to know exactly how serious I was.

She stood up, her purse in hand, walking toward me. "B...but, what are you...I thought we were..."

"We were fucking," I said bluntly. "Yeah, we fucked a couple of times, but I never said I was looking for anything more. I never led you on. I never asked you on a date, brought you flowers, called you, or even acted the least bit excited that you showed up at my door without calling."

Carla squared her shoulders and gathered herself. I could tell the words had stung her, but after so many attempts to get the hint of the last month, I didn't feel bad in the least. I was absolving myself of the guilt. This was not my fault.

Carla pushed her chin up in the air and pursed her lips together. "You are a selfish, arrogant bastard. That's what you fucking are!"

I shrugged. At least she got me.

Her heels clicked against the marble floors as she stomped down the hallway toward the front door. I followed at a safe distance behind her, just to make sure that she was actually going to leave my apartment.

She flung open the door and dramatically turned back toward me. "You are going to end up alone, Silas Denton. You wouldn't know a good thing if it hit you in the face."

I smiled at her and nodded. "And that is absolutely okay with me. Thanks. Bye bye."

She threw her hands up with a huff and slammed the door behind her. I walked gingerly over and locked the top lock, just for good measure. Turning, my scotch still in my hand, I took a deep breath and reveled in the silence. I could finally relax.

I loosened my tie and rolled my sleeves up to my elbows as I walked back to my den and sat on the couch. Despite the large family I had, I'd always been by myself, and I was okay with that. We were all incredibly different, and putting us in one space never turned out well.

I put my feet up on the glass coffee table and reached for the cigar case beside me. Nothing like whiskey and a cigar at the end of a long successful day. Oh, and silence, that was more valuable than all of it.

4

IRIS

When my shift at the café was over, I cheerfully wished everyone a good evening, and headed over to the organization temporary headquarters. At the time, I only had two other people coming in on a daily basis. They worked as hourly employees with the occasional bonus here and there for their hard work. I wanted to do what I could to keep them, but offering them a salary was not possible just yet. They didn't work alone though, I had a handful of volunteers who showed up here and there to offer what they could.

My two dedicated full time girls were Naomi and Sarah. They were both good friends, Naomi having been my best friend for a long time. We were completely different, our background, our status in life, our outlook on things, but we always worked so well. She really had no personal reason to dedicate herself to the cause, having grown up without ever knowing the effects of addiction and drug abuse, but because the charity was important to me, she dedicated herself to it. Naomi might have been my opposite, but her heart was golden. She had been the glue that kept me together and I wasn't sure what I would do without her.

Every time I mentioned a salary, or the lack thereof, Naomi was always quick to point out that she didn't need it. It was true, her family was loaded, but I knew how much she hated asking for money from her parents. I knew her time and skills would be way better served if she actually worked at building her career. But instead, she dedicated her time to working with me and helping build the agency.

Naomi was waiting excitedly for me brimming with good news. As I walked through the door, I could tell her and Sarah had been discussing whatever it was, and they both jumped up excitedly when they saw me.

"Guess what Naomi did?" Sarah asked as I put my bag down.

Naomi blushed a little but she wasn't able to keep the good news a secret for very long. "We're going to have a fundraiser. The biggest one yet!"

I loved the sound of it already. "An actual fundraiser?"

Naomi nodded, walking over to my desk. "Yeah, with rich people who'd be willing to donate a lot of money."

With a smile on my lips, I scrunched my brow, glancing over at Sarah. "Where?"

Naomi licked her lips and calmed herself, pressing her hand to her stomach. "I got my dad to agree to book the Club and invite all his friends, and their friends, and so on. It's going to be huge."

My mouth dropped open and I sat there stunned for a minute. Sarah giggled, bringing my mind out of the shock. I stood up and laughed, coming around the desk and wrapping Naomi in a huge hug. "So, you're going to say yes?" she asked.

I nodded wildly. "Of course I am."

Usually, I was quick to refuse any kind of monetary help from Naomi, even though I knew her family could afford it. At the end of the day, I wanted the agency to be a success based on *our* hard work, not because I was best friends with a woman whose family was rich. But the prospect of a huge fundraiser at a fancy club with rich attendees wasn't something I could pass up. Especially since my personal deadline of building an actual physical center by the end of the year was coming up very soon.

"This is going to be a huge success," Sarah said wrapping her arms around the both of us.

Naomi nodded. "We'll raise a lot of money, Iris, I promise. We're going to get you that building. Maybe it'll be big enough for a dorm *and* a cafeteria!"

Naomi and Sarah were just as excited as I was, and I couldn't stop hugging them. I had tears in my eyes. Despite my apprehension in the past to that kind of crowd, I knew that the party could lead to something big, something beautiful.

"Okay, okay, let's take a deep breath," I suggested, stepping back and taking in a deep breath. "We can discuss the fundraiser tomorrow. Today we have to deal with the newcomers."

I'd already seen a handful of women outside in the waiting area and they had to be our first priority. When we got new clients, usually women who walked in off the street, or heard about us through the grapevine, one of us always took the time to sit down with them on an individual basis. We wanted to get to know them, see what their motivations were, discuss all the options they had at their disposal. Leaving them sitting in the waiting room for too long was never a good idea. Most of them were either in the beginning of detoxing, or they were using and when the drugs wore off, they would leave before ever getting to speak to someone.

Sarah, Naomi, and I got to work but I knew each of us was thinking about the fundraiser in the back of our minds. I thought about all the ways we could utilize the money we made. How many more women and families we could help, how many lives we could save. It was an excitement that I wasn't used to. We were used to the other shoe dropping over and over again, making do with what we had. This was different.

By nine that night we had spoken to the last client, and I hugged Sarah and Naomi goodbye, thanking them for everything. They were going out, but my focus was on Bess. She had been at the neighborhood daycare center all day. It was a small privately owned place, and she could stay there late whenever I had to run an evening shift at the organization. I tried not to work late, but with only Naomi and Sarah, I ended up staying until nine or ten two to three times a week.

Bess never complained. She always reassured me that daycare was a lot of fun. Besides, I trusted Molly and the care she provided the kids under her wing.

"She was an angel as usual," Molly said, walking Bess to the door.

"Bye, Miss Molly." Bess reached up, giving Molly a big hug.

"Thanks," I grinned. "See you tomorrow."

I took Bess's hand and we headed down the block. She swung her little arm forward and back. "Were there more ladies for you to help today, Mommy?"

Bess had always been so proud of me for what I did with the organization. I had always been open and honest with her about what we did, and I talked openly about drug abuse with her. It wasn't to scare her, it was to educate her so that she would grow up knowing the dangers.

"There were a few ladies who came in today. Naomi, Sarah, and I worked with them. Hopefully they'll be able to get the professional help they need," I told her.

Bess wrapped her arms tightly around me and I stroked her hair as we walked.

"Can I be just like you when I grow up?" she asked. I felt myself choke a little as I tried to speak.

"You should aspire to be so much more, my sweetheart. You *will* be so much more, Bessy. I know it. I can just feel it in my bones. You're going to be a wonderful successful kind young woman," I said, and I truly believed it.

I didn't know what other surprises I had in store in my own life, but I wanted my daughter's to be nothing less than amazing.

5

SILAS

Dad had asked for me to meet him at his office when I was done with my conference call. It was slightly unusual. He rarely asked for a meeting, and if he had something, he needed to talk to me about, he usually came to me.

I hung up the phone and emailed the notes over to my secretary to organize. It was a call with our associates in Japan. We were working on a large scale condo project there as well, and I had to make sure everything stayed on track. I didn't like surprises, especially when I couldn't just hop in a taxi and head to the site.

"Lena, I sent over the notes," I called to her as I walked toward the door. "Hold my calls, I'm going down to my father's office."

"Yes, Mr. Denton," she yelled after me.

His secretary held the door open for me and I smiled as I side stepped into his office. He was standing at the window, staring out at the city skyline.

"Everything okay?" I asked.

He hadn't wanted to talk about the company in over a

year so anytime he called me down I was amped and ready, hoping he was picking up steam. It wasn't unusual to find him staring out of his window at odd times of the day, though.

I was concerned for him, but we didn't share the kind of relationship where I could ask him to talk to me. I respected him, I was proud to have him as my father, and I wished my brothers felt the same way about him—but my relationship with my father was far from cozy.

He turned toward me at the sound of my voice and for a moment, he looked as if he had forgotten he had called me down at all. After a few seconds though, he snapped his fingers and walked over to his desk. "Oh yes, everything's fine. Why would it not be? I just got word from Jason Devalo about a charity fundraiser at the Club."

He shuffled a few things and then clapped his hands together as he walked over to the pristine white couch in the middle of his tastefully designed office. I knew my father didn't really care for the office either, but certain appearances needed to be maintained.

"Okay, what kind of a fundraiser is it?" I asked, while he poured himself a dark rich espresso from a pot.

Dad took a sip of his coffee, and this time he sighed deeply. His shoulders squared and he had a forlorn expression on his face. "It's for some anti-drugs nonprofit, based on the Southside."

"Anti-drug?" I asked, my shoulders stiffening, surprised that my father was even bringing this up after everything that had happened.

He stared at me squarely. "That's right."

He gave me a moment to take it all in before continuing. "I think we should attend, I would like you to represent the company. The family."

I clenched my jaw and pushed my hands into the pockets of my tailored pants. "Do you think it would be wise to make a public statement like that?"

I watched my father's nostrils flare. I knew that reaction all too well. He was about to snap at me. "Who is going to say anything to us? You think anyone has the balls? Are you going to pussy out of this, son?"

His cup quivered in his hand as he growled at me. I knew how to handle his bouts of rage. I just remained silent and said nothing. I gave him a moment to gather himself and, of course, eventually he did.

He tugged the bottom of his suit jacket and cleared his throat. "I believe it would be advantageous to our family's name and reputation if you attended. If we make a sizable donation to an organization such as this one, it will speak highly to our ability to move forward."

I knew he was right, but I wasn't a fan of making a big public scene. "We could make a silent donation. You could write a check. We don't have to make an appearance."

My father snarled and stood up, slamming his cup down on the side table. "I don't want to have to say this again, Silas. You are going. We made a decision four years ago, do you remember? We made a pact. It's time we honor the terms of that pact."

"There are other ways of doing it," I grunted and he shook his head.

"We owe this," was all he replied.

From the quiet tone in which his words came out, I knew now that our argument was finished. Dad was putting his foot down and I would have no choice but to execute his wishes.

I said nothing, just turned and walked to the door.

"I'll have my girl give your girl the details," I heard him call out to me as I headed out of his office.

Why was it that, even though I was the only person in this family who had stood by him through all this, through all those years, I was still the person picking up the pieces for him?

I banged my office door shut behind me and stormed over to my desk. From the corner of my eye I'd seen Lena stand up to say something but she'd seen the bullish look on my face and knew that meant I did not want to be disturbed.

I was frustrated and angry, feeling that were all too common for me when it came to my father. I stood by the man because for some twisted fucking reason, I still looked up to him. Despite everything that I knew about him, everything I had helped him achieve, helped him fix, and this was how he repaid me. I had to be his henchman, do his dirty work.

If he wanted to donate to that fucking agency so bad, then why wasn't he the one attending the fundraiser? Why was he going to make me do it?

Didn't he realize this money was tainted? That our family would always be tainted? That giving away money to charity was never going to solve the shitstorm we'd brewed.

That *he* had brewed?

It was nearly impossible to walk into a fundraiser like the one I was being ordered to attend, and still keep my head held up high.

I paced around my office, feeling the stress of everything flooding over me. All the excitement for the new project, the new beginning was hidden behind a sea of past emotions. Eventually, I sat down behind my desk with my head in my hands.

Why did I stay when everyone else left?

I should have done the same thing my brothers did. Packed up my shit and zipped.

For some reason, I continued to believe that our father deserved a second chance. That he deserved a new lease on life.

Was I wrong? His past was eventually going to catch up with him, with us, right?

6
IRIS

*E*veryone was excited about the fundraiser, but Bess' excitement was in a league of its own. Obviously it being an upscale venue we were going to have to dress up for it, she was going to be allowed to stay up late, and we were going to a luxurious, fancy Club. This was going to be her first real party.

I tried to explain the details to her, but being just six years old, she didn't fully understand the gravity of the event. It had the potential to change the future of my organization. Despite that, Bess knew it was a big deal.

I bought Bess a new dress to wear because she deserved it. It was a frilly purple frock with a matching silver and purple bow for her hair. She looked adorable in it and spent most of the evening staring at herself in the mirror. Normally I would remind her that it wasn't about the clothes she wore, it was about the content of her character, her morals, and her heart, but for that one night, I let her feel beautiful inside and out.

I couldn't afford to spend any more money on clothes for myself, so I dug through my closet, pulling out the nicest dress that I owned. It was a deep teal cocktail dress that I had worn years before to a wedding. It had always fit me perfectly with a conservative but sexy lace neckline. The A-line shape of the dress accentuated my curvy hips and hid any parts of me I tended to wince at when walking past the mirror after a shower. I figured it was classic enough to not look outdated even though fashion hadn't been on my radar in a very long time.

The event was going to be sophisticated and classy. That was what Naomi's family was all about and expected nothing less from the party.

Laying my black heels on the bed next to my satin black clutch, Bess' watched with a twinkle in her eye. For the first time in months, I spent more than a just few minutes on my hair and makeup. Bess followed me into the bathroom and I set her up on the counter next to me. She swung her legs, watching every stroke of my brush, every twirl of the curling iron, and every splash of color I applied to my lips.

"I love curls," she giggled as I let my hair fall in soft waves around my shoulders.

"Me too, little one," I replied with a wink.

She watched as applied another coat of lipstick, my face shimmering in a classic natural look.

"Wow, Mommy, you look beautiful!" Bess declared as I did a little walk for her, twirling at the end for good measure.

Her awe-inspired tone made me laugh and I realized I was actually blushing.

"And you look like a princess, my darling baby," I said and I covered her face with kisses

The doorbell rang and Bess went running. Naomi was at the door. She'd come over to give us a ride to the Club.

"Look at you two!" Naomi was genuinely excited to see us both.

Bess ran into her arms and they twirled in circles. As she set Bess down, Naomi looked up at me, skimming over my outfit. She gave me a playful wink and I rolled my eyes, shaking my head. Naomi looked effortlessly sexy as always. Sometimes I couldn't figure out how *we* were best friends!

"Your chariot awaits, my lady!" She bowed to Bess, taking her hand as she giggled.

"I can't begin to tell you how nervous I am right now," I whispered into Naomi's ear as we left my apartment.

Riding along in Naomi's car, I drummed my fingers anxiously on my knee.

"Why are you nervous, Iris?" she asked over the sound of the radio.

Bess was in the back, looking excitedly out of the window.

I glanced back to make sure she wasn't paying attention. I wanted to always be strong and brave in her eyes. "What if nobody donates? What if my presentation isn't good enough? I feel like you've put your neck on the line, strong-armed your dad into doing us this favor, and I'm going to end up disappointing everyone. At the end of the day, these people are going to have to buy what I'm selling, right?"

Naomi sighed with a warm smile on her lips. "First of all, everyone is going to donate. I can't make promises on how much, but none of them are showing up to this thing with an empty wallet. These people, my dad's friends and acquaintances have too much money and not enough things to spend it on. Donating to a charity like ours is considered fashionable."

Naomi was rolling her eyes as she spoke. I knew she didn't care much for her family's money or the way they often acted like they were better than everyone else. "And secondly, these people just need an excuse to get dressed up and come to the club. If they didn't come for a fundraiser, it would have been for something. And most importantly, I think you're going to sell the shit out of it. These people might be coming tonight just for sport, but they won't know what hit them when they see your beautiful face and hear your powerful words."

I smiled at her and she smiled back, reaching over patting my hand. "Don't be nervous, you're going to be fine."

"It's my first official fundraiser. I don't even know if I can do something like this." I had a speech prepared in my purse for later, which I'd memorized, but I felt like I'd already forgotten all the words to it.

"I'll be there with you the whole time," Naomi insisted.

I looked away and out of the window as we zoomed through the city, leaving the southside behind. If we were able to raise enough money for a brand new location, we would actually be able to start housing people overnight at our facility. The women who were trying to get clean or get away from other drug users, would have somewhere to spend the night. They wouldn't have to go back home or go to a clinic waiting facility or a subpar rehab facility. They could wait until the right option opened for them. They could feel safe with us for one night, two nights, however many nights they needed. It would be a very beneficial service to provide.

Trying to keep the nerves away, I daydreamt about all the different things we could do with the money, even though I had no real idea how much we were actually going to raise.

All I could do was be thankful for Naomi and for having

her support. I wouldn't have been able to do any of it if it wasn't for her.

Helping people, running an organization like this wasn't just a dream anymore.

"We're here!" I heard her say.

I glanced out the window, raising my eyebrows as we pulled up a long manicured drive toward an opulent white building ahead. Bess gasped and giggled in the back seat while I swallowed down the intimidation that quickly crept up my spine. I had never even been close to a place like that, but ready or not, I was about to take control of it.

7

SILAS

Walking into the Club, I noticed the long line of cars parked out in the driveway. It was the kind of Club that my father had eyed enviously for years, wanting desperately be accepted as a member. Year after year, though, the board rejected his application, finding him "unsuitable for membership." After being in business for decades, he struggled to be part of the cool kid club. Luckily for the rest of us who were tired of hearing him grump about it, two years before he had finally gotten his acceptance letter. He was part of the rich guy club.

Along with the fact that we ran the most profitable real estate agency in Chicago, his membership to this Club had to be on the top of his list of achievements. And yet, he did not want to attend the fundraiser himself. So, there I was, walking inside, taking one for the team...forefully. Maybe my brothers were right after all, maybe our father didn't deserve my support.

In my suit and my leather shoes, carrying a massive check in my wallet, I pushed forward, always being the dutiful son. I wasn't obsessed with being the "golden child,"

I didn't want to abandon our father whose health, both mental and physical, was no longer strong and full of vitality.

As I followed the signs through the club to the East Ballroom, I nodded at a few friendly faces walking past. At the door, two women, middle aged, dressed as nice as they could, handed me a brochure as I entered.

Chicago Anti-Drug: Fighting drug abuse as a community. Families helping families.

I stepped to the side, right inside the ballroom, wondering why I had never heard of the organization before. I flicked quickly through the brochure, finding that it was a fairly new organization. As a matter of fact, it was still at its infancy at just two years old. That made sense as to why I'd never heard of it before.

The brochure was filled with interesting statistics and information on the drug scene in Chicago, particularly in the Southside of the city, and how it was affecting families. Nothing in the brochure was information I wasn't already aware of. Unfortunately, none of it was news to me, but I tucked it into the inside pocket of my jacket anyway.

A server walked past me with a tray of champagne and I picked up a crystal flute. The only thing that was going to get me through that night would be lots and lots of alcohol.

I smiled at the familiar faces who smiled at me, but I had no intention of making actual conversation with anyone. The plan was to stay long enough that people saw my face, saw me making the contribution at the donation stand, shake a few hands, and then I'd leave.

That way, my father could feel included in his little club he thought he was a part of. The club I knew would never accept him as their own because he was always going to be an outsider to them.

I stood to the side by myself, ignoring the glances from the women who showed just to brag about their thousand dollar dresses and diamonds. Women who would never have a clue what the organization they were supporting really did. Nor would they ever truly care.

I was ploughing down the champagne, eventually just ignoring everyone. When I finished one glass, I looked up to find the waiter. As I scanned the crowd, my eyes landed on a woman standing on the other side of the room. She stood, smiling, making conversation with two middle aged men, Rolexes on their wrists, balding, and bulging waist lines.

She felt familiar, but not because I ever thought I had met her before. I could tell she was an outsider, just like me, just like my father. There was something about the way she moved, the simplicity of her dress, the way her smile was polite but distant. I saw right through her.

But my focus fell on her for the same reason a dozen of other men were staring, she was gorgeous. Her aura was alluring, and you could tell she wasn't even trying to be that way. She might even be completely oblivious to it.

She had a curvy profile, big breasts, and wide hips. The dress she wore fit snugly to her figure, accentuating her allure, and creating a seductive sway to her ass. Her hair was dark, wavy, and fell around her shoulders, nearly reaching her waist. I kept picturing winding her hair around my hand and gently tugging her head back while I took her from behind.

I shouldn't have been having those thoughts about a woman I knew nothing about and who seemed to have no idea how lustfully the men around her were staring, but I couldn't help it.

Why was she here?

She didn't belong with any of those people. She didn't

belong to the club either. She looked just as out of place as I felt.

And then it struck me. She worked for the organization. She was trying to raise money for the charity. How perfect could my luck be?

I had a check in my pocket, a membership to the club, and the perfect excuse to talk to her. I had never needed an excuse to talk to a woman before, but she made me nervous, clammy. I felt compelled to be closer as if her very existence drew me in. I swallowed the last sips of my champagne, straightened my jacket, and headed straight for her.

8

IRIS

I was trying to educate and inform as many people about the work we did at the agency as I could, and it seemed like people were really listening. Naomi, Sarah, and a few other volunteers were there with me, doing the rounds and talking about our work.

I'd taught Bess a few lines too, so she was charming the guests as well, but mostly she was hanging around with Naomi who was introducing her to all her father's friends.

The more time I spent talking to those people, the less intimidated I felt. I would have to go up on the stage and make a short speech at some point, urging everyone to donate generously. At first that had been the most stressful part of the whole night, but after actually interacting with everyone, realizing they were people too, I wasn't so nervous. I was beginning to think I might actually make it through the night without any major hiccups.

I was in the middle of telling a couple middle aged men, their money almost bursting from their pockets, about the plans I had for the money raised that night. As I spoke, I caught movement from the corner of my eye. I looked up and saw *him*. Despite the fact that I was in the middle of a sentence, I couldn't look away from him. There was a strange knowing grin on his face like he knew exactly the effect he had on women. He could sense me, an animal hunting his prey, and I found it both strange and erotic at the same time.

It wasn't often that a man had such a knee-weakening effect on me. I felt like my throat was closing up and I was painfully aware of the sudden desire that coursed through my veins.

At first sight, there was absolutely nothing about this man I could fault. He had the most incredibly delicious bone structure. Chiseled jaw, a sharp Roman nose, and sparkling blue eyes. His dark hair was slick and brushed stylishly back. I could almost imagine myself running my fingers through it, gripping onto it...

That dark tailored suit clung to his body. The perfected tailoring of every seam accentuated his strong thighs and lean torso. The fabric pulled just slightly at the bicep, and I felt a compulsive need to grab him by the blue satin tie and pull him to me.

I shook my head, trying to jerk my mind out of the more than embarrassing thoughts. I realized that one of the gentlemen in front of me was asking me a question. "Oh, I'm sorry. What were you saying?"

"I was just commenting on how adorable your daughter is. She's going to end up raising a lot of the money here tonight," he said with a chuckle.

I had to drag my gaze away from that man. The one who'd blown my senses away with some sort of other-worldly sex appeal. I was hoping that he had disappeared magically into thin air. That maybe he was just a figment of my imagination. It sure felt like it could have been. I didn't think there were really people out that perfect.

"Gentlemen, do you mind if I steal this lovely young lady away from you for a moment?"

I didn't even need to turn around to know that magic was not playing any part in my night. Just the tone of his voice sent chills down my spine. He stepped up next to me, putting his hand on the small of my back. My whole body went stiff.

He stepped to the side, a wide step, to get away from the two men I'd been talking to, and I had no choice but to do the same. My heart was racing. I had no idea what I would say. I'd forgotten all my talking points.

"Hi, we haven't been introduced yet," I said, trying to make somewhat of a conversation.

His gaze traveled up and down, taking in my body, assessing every curve and turn of me. I felt thoroughly scrutinized, like it was a job interview of some kind.

"No, we haven't. You seem to be associated with the charity, if I'm not mistaken," he replied

"I'm Iris Neilson. I'm the founder," I said and extended a hand to him.

I was just glad my hand wasn't shaking. He took a second to think before he actually shook it. I felt an electric wave run through my body when we touched. Like he was cursing me, playing some voodoo trick on my mind.

I couldn't remember the last time a man had that effect on me. Was it really all because of the way he looked, or was there something else about him that was pulling me in?

"Silas." As he said his name, I unconsciously licked my lips.

"I would love to tell you more about our agency, unless you have already thought of some questions for me. And thank you for accepting our invitation to this fundraiser."

I was trying to run through my prepared lines, but I was aware of how harsh and rehearsed they sounded. He didn't seem to care though. He was smiling. He'd withdrawn his hand and tucked it in the pocket of his pants. I brushed a hand through my hair and tried to think of other things to say. He just stared at me though, not answering, not replying, just staring.

"Okay, so if you don't have any questions, I can just start by telling you a little about the kind of work we do."

I was about to add more but he interrupted me.

He shook his head. "Let me just stop you there, Iris. I am perfectly aware of the work you and your team do. I am aware of the drug situation in the city. You don't have to give me the hard sell."

I thought his tone was a bit rude. He could have at least given me a chance to say something, anything really, instead of interrupting me. My cheeks flushed and I nodded quickly instead.

"Okay," I murmured.

He must have noticed that I looked offended because he took a step towards me, forcing me to look directly up at him, into his deep blue eyes.

"I have a check for you in my pocket," he said.

My brows crossed. What was this about? Where was this conversation going? "Alright, that's extremely generous of you..."

"It's for two hundred-thousand dollars," he added.

I felt my heart skip. I hadn't seen money like that...ever. It was too much. It was plenty. Just his donation alone would be enough to get started on the things that we were planning on doing. Was he serious?

"But there is something I would like you to do for me first," he said.

There was a smile spreading across Silas' face, and a chill ran down my spine. "If this has anything to do with our records, or if you need affirmation of what we're going to do with that money..."

He stopped me again. "I trust you. I'm not concerned about that."

"Then how can I help you?" I asked, searching his eyes.

It wasn't very often that a man made me that nervous. There was certainly something about him that was making me both anxious and intrigued. I swallowed hard and licked my lips again, waiting for an answer from him.

"I would like you to spend this evening with me. As your biggest benefactor, I believe I deserve this special treatment." He nearly looked amused when he said that.

He could see the look of relief in my eyes. I was glad it wasn't some kind of ridiculous request. I didn't even know what to expect from him.

"You want me to spend the evening with you?" I asked in surprise.

He shrugged his wide masculine shoulders. "This is a snooze-fest. No offense to you guys of course, but I can't find one other interesting person here except you. So yes, I would like to spend the rest of the evening with you. And if you really want to, you could even tell me all about your work."

I wasn't loving the sound of amusement in his voice. Like he knew he had me wrapped around his finger. Like he thought I was going to drool at the thought of that check that may or may not have been there in his pocket.

"What makes you think I'd be willing to dedicate all of my time to you? That I don't have better things to do here tonight?" I asked.

He arched his brows in surprise. He wasn't expecting that tone from me. "Are you refusing me?"

I was about to say something more, but Naomi was suddenly in our midst. "Iris! There you are. I've been looking for you. You have to be up on stage. The speech!"

She grabbed my hand and started to drag me away. I exchanged one last look with Silas and he was still smiling. I narrowed my eyes, intrigued by him, flattered by him. He made me feel wanted, important even. As Naomi shoved me up toward the stage, all the fear I had evaporated and my self-confidence took over.

~

My speech went well. Way better than I was expecting it to go. I spoke about our organization's aims and goals, about the things we'd achieved in the past two years, and how many women and families we were able to help and provide a safe place for away from drugs.

I smiled out at the crowd. "There is still so much to do, we are just getting started, and we need everyone's help and support to work together to make our neighborhoods safer for our children, and help Chicago become drug-free."

I didn't mess up my speech like I thought I would, and the whole time I spoke I could see Silas standing in the back watching me. He had one hand gingerly resting in his pocket, and the other holding a glass of champagne. He was so handsome that he stood out in the crowd. I still couldn't wrap my head around his unusual request.

Was that really how rich people behaved? Did they think they could buy anything and anyone with their money?

I should have been offended and angry. I should have snapped at him and told him he couldn't buy me...but I was intrigued. I couldn't deny that flutter of curiosity I felt in my heart when our eyes met.

What did he see in me? This man who could undoubtedly have any woman in the room. Why did he want *my* company?

The speech was over and everyone was clapping. Naomi and Sarah joined me on stage. Naomi made another bid for donations and gave the details to the audience of the many ways that they could donate money to us.

I smiled graciously and stepped off the stage amidst more applause. I wanted to find him again. I had some things to say to him. I tried to make it through the crowd but people kept stopping me and I had to be polite. When I eventually made my way to Silas in the back, I was feeling a bit overwhelmed.

I came to a stop in front of him and crossed my arms over my breasts.

"So, have you made your decision?" he asked with a twinkle in his eye.

I gulped. "Half the evening is over already."

"I'll take what's left of it," he was quick to retort.

"Alright, yes, I'll spend the rest of the time with you," I said.

"Good."

It was like he had a plan in place already. He gave me his arm and I strung mine through it. I started to step forward toward the crowd, but with a quick shift, he pulled me through the doors and away from the ballroom. I glanced back, having no idea where he was taking me. I felt a twinge of panic, and my heart began to race wildly in my chest.

9

SILAS

I wasn't expecting her to accept my offer, especially because of how offended she looked when I first suggested it. I was aware it was crude. I was basically offering her two hundred-thousand dollars in exchange for some time with her. For some reason though, she accepted.

Taking her arm, I lead her out of the ballroom and toward a discreet balcony at the back of the Club.

"Where are we going?" she asked as I pushed open the heavy doors.

"Away from the crowd." I replied with a grin.

We stepped out into the cool air and Iris wrapped her arms around her shoulders. As I unbuttoned my jacket and began to shrug it off, I caught her eyes roving over me. I walked up behind her and gently placed my jacket over her shoulders.

"Is that better?" I asked.

She nodded. "Yes, thank you."

In front of us were the sprawling Club gardens, the trimmed and shaped hedges, and the flowering bushes.

Above us was a shimmering dark sky. It wasn't a very clear night and we lived in a city, but you could still spot glimpses of the universe above us.

"So, what did you want to talk about?" Iris turned to me.

My eyes had adjusted to the dark and I could see her delicate heart-shaped face clearly. She had thick delicious lips that looked bee-stung and kissable. She was wearing a shimmery lip gloss that sparkled in the dim light.

"Nothing in particular." I shrugged.

"So I'm just supposed to find a way to keep you entertained?" she asked with a smile tugging the corners of her lips.

I shrugged again. "Why don't you want to be in there? Aren't they your people?"

That made me laugh. "My people? You make it sound like I belong to some sort of tribe."

"Well, it is a kind of community, isn't it? Rich people." Iris' eyes were wide and she was smiling as she spoke.

I'd known from the beginning' there was something starkly different about her. She wasn't like any other woman I had met. My emotions were all over the place. She was incredibly sexy. I wanted her in my bed. I wanted those clothes to come off of her. But at the same time, I wanted to keep talking to her.

"I can't say I'm an acceptable member of the community you're talking about." My eyes shifted out to the gardens.

"You're not? You had me fooled with that check in your pocket and the clothes you're wearing, and the way people are fawning over you," she replied.

"I'm new to the group," I replied with a laugh.

Her eyes widened and she nodded. "But you're a natural, you fit in well."

I stepped forward and put my hands on the stone rail. "It

doesn't matter, I will always be an outsider. My family will never belong to that Chicago community you're talking about because...because of various other factors."

"*Other* factors?" she asked, raising her brows again.

I didn't want to get into that. I'd already said too much. This conversation was supposed to be flirty and sexy, but somehow it had gotten out of hand.

"What's your story? Why did you start this organization?" I asked, trying to change the subject.

She drew in a deep breath and smiled. "Why do I have to have a story? Isn't it possible that I just want to help and do something good for my neighborhood and this city?"

I stared at her in response, knowingly. There was *story* written all over that face of hers. She was doing a good job of hiding it but I had no doubt she had a past she wasn't speaking about.

"That's fine, you don't have to tell me. We all have our secrets," I told her.

She smiled wider, nodded and looked away.

"So, if this isn't the kind of place you usually like frequenting, why are you here?" Iris continued.

She'd hit another nerve. Why was it so difficult to keep our conversation light and casual? "I had to do this for the sake of my family. They wanted to make a donation, but nobody else was available to attend the fundraiser themselves, so I had to be the representative."

At least that part was entirely true. For a moment I had the urge to just spill everything to her. Iris watched as I took a step towards her. She still had my jacket hanging from her shoulders. She looked up at me but didn't step away. It was obvious that she felt it too—the undeniable sexual chemistry between us. It felt like we were going to set fire to ourselves just by staring at each other.

"What are we really doing here, Silas?" She whispered hoarsely.

I knew she was thinking exactly the same thing I was. "I told you. I wanted to talk to you. I wanted you all to myself."

She lightly bit down on her lower lip and I saw the sparkle of desire in her large green eyes. Did she even know how beautiful she was?

"I'm supposed to be working out there," she continued in a whisper as I reached for her face, brushing a wave of hair away from her cheek.

My fingers grazed her soft skin and she parted her lips. I knew what that meant. She wanted to be kissed and I wanted to kiss her. She had her face turned up at me and I could smell her soft floral perfume.

But then her cellphone rang.

"Oh shit!" she exclaimed, stepping quickly away from me.

She scrambled for it in her purse and fished it out, quickly turning her back to me.

I clenched my jaw in frustration. I was so close to finally kissing her. It had taken me way too long with her than it did with other women. We'd wasted too much time talking.

I heard Iris speaking in monosyllables into the phone. It sounded important.

No fucking way.

No way was I letting her walk away from me!

She was right there in my grasp.

10

IRIS

I was so glad for that phone call because I wasn't sure what I would have ended up doing if it hadn't come through. What was I thinking? Was I seriously going to kiss that man? I didn't know anything about him. I had no idea who he was or what he wanted.

My hand was shaking as I held the phone pressed to my ear. It was Naomi on the line. She and Bess had been looking for me. I told her I'd return to the ballroom straight away. I shouldn't have left Bess alone like that in the first place!

My cheeks were flushed and I felt nervous when I turned around to face him again.

"Work?" He asked casually, as though nothing untoward had happened between us.

My heart was thumping out of my chest! I began to remove his jacket and slowly hand it back to him.

"Kinda, yeah, I should go back in there. I'm sorry but I don't think it'll be possible for me to spend the whole evening cooped up here. There are too many people out there looking for me. My poor daughter has no idea where I am," I said and chuckled lightly.

The look on Silas' face changed drastically when he heard that.

"Your daughter? You have a daughter?" he asked.

I could hear the strain in his voice.

"Y...yes," I admitted, but now it felt like a crime to talk about Bess.

"Wow," he said and ran a hand through his slick perfect hair.

It was like he couldn't believe what he was hearing.

I narrowed my eyes. "I don't understand, is that a problem somehow?"

I had no idea why it was a factor. Me having a daughter... what did that have to do with anything? It wasn't like I'd been keeping crucial information from a man I was in a relationship with. We'd just met!

"I just had no idea. And she's *here*?" he asked, staring at me now like he'd been lied to.

"Yeah, her name is Bess. She's six. You might have seen her around in the ballroom earlier."

Silas nodded gently.

His behavior was pissing me off. Nobody, not even a stunner like him who made me weak in the knees, was going to make me feel guilty about my daughter. I was never going to hide Bess from anybody.

"I don't understand why this is a problem. How does this affect you?" I recognized the snappy tone of my voice and Silas clenched his jaw.

"I don't mean to offend you," he said sourly.

"But you are!"

He rolled his shoulders nonchalantly. "I just had no clue you were a mother. I was going to ask you out."

"And now you're not going to because I have a six year old?" I snapped.

Silas kept his mouth pursed together. I knew he wasn't going to reply to that question. It didn't matter. If that was the kind of man he was, who would have a problem with my daughter—then there was no way I could get into any kind of a relationship with him anyway.

I shook my head in dismay and I whipped away from him.

"Iris!" He growled my name as I strode to the door. "Please take the check."

I turned to him slowly again. The last thing I wanted to do was accept anything from him. My blood was boiling under my skin. I wanted to scream at him for making me feel that way. He acted like Bess was some kind of baggage.

I watched in silence as he pulled the check out of his pocket and held it out towards me. "It's not like you can refuse my donation. I'll hand it over to one of your colleagues if you don't take it from me right now. Let's just make this easier for us. You take the check from me now, I walk out of here, and you never have to see me again."

He had a point. I snapped the check out of his hands and opened my purse dropping it in. "Goodnight, Silas."

I didn't wait to hear another word from him. I could sense him watching me as I walked off the balcony and rushed down the corridor. I tried to find my way back to the ballroom

My heart was still racing.

He was a strange man. Was he really thinking of asking me out? Why me? I still didn't understand it. Either way, I was glad the point about Bess came out before I actually agreed to go out with him. I knew I would have accepted his offer to take me out. I was so close to kissing him already.

The past six years had all been about Bess. I'd barely dated, but now, when I saw Silas...I knew I was ready again. I could feel it in my whole body. When I stepped into the ballroom, I saw that Bess and Naomi were waiting there for me. Bess ran into my arms and I hugged her tight.

"Sorry honey, I got carried away talking to someone outside," I told her.

Naomi came over, smiling too. "We've already had a number of high profile donations. You did good on stage earlier."

I was going to tell her about the check in my purse, but decided I'd tell her later when we were tallying the money raised. I needed to calm myself about Silas first, so that Naomi didn't detect something fishy when I spoke about him.

I held Bess' hand and we started walking around the ballroom, mingling again. It might not have seemed like much to Silas, but the whole party was a lot of work for me. I was actually trying to get something accomplished, something bigger than clubs and rich people.

It didn't matter though...like he said, I would probably never have to see him again.

11

SILAS

I stormed out of the Club and headed straight for my Cadillac. It was insane. Why was I feeling that way? I'd accomplished what Dad wanted me to. I'd attended the fundraiser, handed over the check, made my presence known, and I was leaving.

I stood at the valet stand, tapping my foot, grinding my teeth. I glanced back at the club several times, feeling like I had been pushed out, and not even by one of the members. The valet pulled my car up and got out. As I reached for the handle, I paused, staring back at the building. I let out a deep breath and turned, tossing my tag back to the valet. "I'll be right back."

Hadn't I done the right thing?

Before I could get three steps away, I stopped again, realizing that going back in there was a stupid idea. I had already made myself known, I had already made her think I was a complete jerk. Standing on the balcony, I was going to ask her out, or ask her to come home with me...but neither of those options would have been viable given that Iris had a daughter.

That was strictly against my rules. I couldn't let myself get involved with a woman who had a child. No matter how short-lived that relationship was going to be. A kid just always complicated everything.

Shaking my head, I turned back and got in my car, tipped the valet, and roared out of the driveway into the night. I felt like I was trying to get as far away from the Club as possible. That was exactly why I never liked to attend those events. They always led to unnecessary complications.

Driving back to my penthouse with the music on loud, all I could really do was think about Iris. I was fantasizing about her. How that kiss would have tasted if we hadn't been interrupted by that stupid phone call.

If I had her in my arms, if I'd been able to just feel her body against mine, I would have had something to bank on. Before she told me about her daughter, that was.

I stopped at a red light and rubbed a hand frustratedly over my face.

Fuck. Fuck. Fuck!

Why couldn't I get her out of my head?

It was just sex. I desired her body. I wanted her in my bed. I could have that with a dozen other gorgeous women who were waiting for me to call them back. What was it about this one that I couldn't let go of?

Was it because I hadn't even gotten a taste of her? Because she'd managed to keep me on my toes? Keep me guessing?

The light changed to green and I zoomed ahead again.

But she hated me. She'd seen the look of horror on my face when I learned that she had a kid. It was obvious that I'd offended her. It was natural. I had no right to make her feel bad because she had a child.

The only person I could blame for my frustration was myself.

I gripped the steering wheel hard.

Maybe I needed to fuck someone else. That would get her out of my mind. *Yeah. Good idea. Fuck someone else.*

~

I walked into my apartment and threw my car keys to the side, paying no attention to where they landed.

As much as I tried to get her out of mind, try to pick one of the existing women from my pool of options, I couldn't. Iris was all I could fantasize about. I tried to make myself comfortable on the couch, turning on the television and flipping through the channels. After about five minutes of that though, I clicked it off and dropped the remote in the floor. There wasn't a single thing on tv that was entertaining enough to take my mind away from that woman.

Should I have stayed? Should I have watched her all night and then asked her to come back here with me after the night was over?

What about her kid? She had her kid there at the fundraiser with her!

Was she really looking for a one-night stand?

In my experience, women with children were not the kind of women who were looking for fun without strings attached. They had too much going on in their lives, they had their kids to think about.

But Iris was about to kiss me if it hadn't been for that phone call. She barely knew me. We'd met just an hour before. If she was willing to kiss me, how much farther was she willing to go? Was I willing to go farther than a one night stand?

I couldn't stop visualizing a date with her. Somewhere understated but still classy. Somewhere she could wear another short and clingy cocktail dress to. I was picturing sitting across from her, hearing her speak, smile at me with that twinkle in her wide green eyes.

I threw my head back and stared up at the ceiling. I couldn't deny it anymore. Iris Neilson had most definitely cast a spell on me. I couldn't remember any other woman having that desperate of an effect on me.

It was like I was going mad. I had to see her again.

12

IRIS

We drove back toward the southside with Bess asleep in the backseat. It was nearly midnight. The event had gone way better than I could have hoped for. I knew it was a huge success and even though we hadn't tallied the exact number, there was no doubt that we had enough to get started, to really make a difference with the work we were doing.

We were both really excited, gabbing back and forth I hadn't realized what a high something like that could be. To actually have so many people come up to me and tell me what a good job we were doing, it was wild. It made everything worthwhile. I'd started off the agency based on nothing but a desire to help people and it was finally beginning to feel like it was getting off the ground. That all the things I sacrificed and all the time I spent away from my daughter might pay off.

Naomi was gushing and so was I, but Silas and that check in my purse were constantly in the back of my mind. I hadn't yet told Naomi about the two-hundred thousand dollars we could add to our tally.

Finally, there was a lull in our conversation so I opened my purse and I pulled it out. Holding the check in my fingers, I could still feel the warmth of Silas standing next to me.

I shook the thought away and forced a smile on my face. "Oh, I almost forgot about this other donation that came in."

"Oh yeah?" Naomi looked at me as I pulled the check out of my purse.

I couldn't bring myself to meet her gaze. "You know when you couldn't find me? One of the men at the event took me aside. He wanted to talk about the agency, find out more about our work and all that. Then he handed me this check."

I waved it in front of my face, feeling a little guilty that I was fabricating a story to my best friend. I just felt like if I told her about Silas, I would have to admit to the fact that I had forgotten for just a moment that I was a mom, a friend, a responsible adult. That I had agreed to spend the evening with a man that I didn't even know. How I had almost let myself be lost in his kiss.

None of those things were points I wanted to discuss at that moment. I knew it would be best if I just forgot all about him.

"How much is it?" Naomi asked, interrupting my thoughts.

I licked my lips and looked down at the handwriting on the check. He hadn't lied.

"Two hundred thousand dollars." I said the words in a slow soft voice.

"Oh my God! Are you serious? That is some serious dough, Iris!" Naomi was squealing with excitement.

But I wasn't smiling anymore. I was still staring down at the check in my hands. I was reading the rest of the check.

"Who is he? The man who gave you this check?" Naomi asked.

My voice was shaky and my eyes were wide with shock as I looked up at my friend. She was driving, trying to keep her eyes on the road but when she glanced at me she knew something was wrong.

"Iris? What? Who gave you this check?" she asked.

I gulped. The words were stuck in my throat.

"The Denton family."

∼

Naomi didn't get it. She kept driving, clueless as to why my reaction had been so full of shock.

"The Denton family? You mean the real estate people? The guys who built the..."

I interrupted her. "Yes, them."

Naomi shrugged. "That's great isn't it? I mean, why does it matter who he is? It's great that you made an impression and he wrote a check for that much. Oh my God, I seriously still can't believe it."

She chuckled while she drove, and of course, she had every right to be excited. I should have been just as jubilant, but I couldn't, not when I knew what I knew.

I clutched the check tightly with both hands and stared down at it. Silas had a neat hand, slanted and refined. I understood everything he said, what he meant when he said he was never going to be accepted by the Club and the society of traditional rich people in the city.

"I didn't need to make an impression on him. He came with the check in his pocket. He already knew he was going to donate and how much he was going to give," I said dryly.

"Okay, fine, whatever. So, they wanted to make a donation, maybe they've heard of us, maybe they actually care about the work we do. It doesn't matter, Iris. I told you. These people all have money and they don't know what to do with it. Good for us. Why does it look like this is bothering you?"

Naomi was trying to sell it to me, but no matter what she said, it was not going to take away the huge lump that had settled in the pit of my stomach.

His name was Silas Denton.

I nearly kissed Silas Denton...what was I thinking? Why didn't I ask him his last name? Did he know I would have recognized him? Was it all some kind of twisted ploy?

"Whatever the reason is, Iris, it's good money and we should be happy about it," Naomi continued to speak even though I hadn't replied to her in some time.

Finally, I snapped my head around to look at her. "They didn't give us this money because they believe in our cause or think we do good work, Naomi. They've given us this money because they feel guilty!"

She had her brows crossed in confusion. "Guilty how? What are you talking about, Iris?"

"The Denton family. They ran one of the biggest drug scenes in the Southside until four years ago. They are part of the fucking problem we are still trying to solve!"

13

SILAS

I worked until six the next day in the office before I cracked. Lena looked like she was in shock when she saw me stepping out of the office, ready to leave.

"Are you headed for a meeting, Mr. Denton?" she asked, jumping off her chair.

"No, I'm calling it a day," I replied, walking right past her.

She still couldn't believe it. She'd never seen me leaving the office that early unless I had a business obligation to keep. "Is there..."

I shook my head. "No, there is absolutely nothing for you to do here, Lena. You should go home too."

The elevator doors pinged open and I stepped in. When I turned around, I saw her standing there, staring at me like she'd been slapped, like she had no idea what she was supposed to do with her new found time.

Before I left the office, I had looked up the address of the agency that Iris founded. It was going to be easy to find. I was familiar enough with the neighborhood.

I'd spent the whole day thinking about her. I'd fantasized about her right through two conference calls and one board meeting. Not even my dad, praising my expertise with the new construction deal at the meeting was able to capture my attention. All I could think about was Iris in that teal dress, her angelic hair, her shimmery bee-stung lips, and those green eyes staring longingly at me.

Would I have to grovel? I would need to apologize, I knew that much. I shouldn't have reacted the way I did to the news of the existence of her daughter. I might have to work a little harder than expected but I knew she wouldn't be able to hold out for very long. None of the women could. Especially not one who was so close to kissing me. She was half cracked already. I was pretty sure she had stayed up all night fantasizing about me too.

So even though I knew I had to apologize to her, I was still feeling pretty good. I was going to score that night. I was going to whisk her away from that place, take her to some classy cocktail bar, and then drive her to my place where I could take her clothes off one piece at a time.

By the time I was done, she wouldn't know what hit her.

If there was one thing I didn't doubt, it was my ability to bed a beautiful woman. Iris might have been a little extraordinary, but there was nothing about her that intimidated me, nothing about her I couldn't handle.

I got into my Cadillac and my engine roared. I was ready to drive over to the old hood. Southside. I even felt a little tingle in my fingers. I hadn't been back there in four years and my desire for a woman was what was dragging me back. It would be comical if it wasn't so tragic.

I parked outside the small old building and saw that the front door was wide open. They were clearly trying to make a point about their open door policy.

I buttoned my suit jacket and walked straight in, hoping to see Iris. Instead, I saw a different woman first. She had the air of someone who worked there and was talking to woman who seemed to be in need of help. They both turned to look at me.

The woman who appeared to be part of the operation smiled, squeezed the other's hand, and stepped toward me. "Hi, I'm Naomi. How can I help you?"

"Hi, I'm looking for Iris Neilson. Is she here today?" I asked.

I looked around the place. It didn't seem like much. It was a small establishment with a small cramped waiting area and what seemed like two other rooms. Naomi was looking me up and down curiously. "Sure, yeah, she's just in there with a few people. I wouldn't want to disturb her while she's in the middle of her counseling unless it's an absolute emergency."

"That's okay, I can wait," I replied.

Naomi gave me a hesitant smile. "Great, I'm sure she'll be out soon if you would like to have a seat."

There were a few plastic chairs in the waiting area and I started walking toward them.

"Sorry, may I ask what this is about?" Naomi followed me.

I unbuttoned my jacket, not even looking at her as I spoke. "Nothing official. I just need to speak to her about something personal."

She looked unconvinced. I wasn't sure who she was, but

I was starting to think that it was quite possible she was someone who knew Iris pretty well.

"Something personal? What is your name, if you don't mind me asking?" she continued.

I wasn't sure if I wanted to tell her my name. It was likely that if that woman was close friends with Iris, then she would have filled her in on my reaction about her daughter.

"Look, is it okay if I just wait here for Iris? I won't be taking up much of her time. I just need to say something to her," I insisted.

Maybe it wasn't going to be so easy to get Iris to come on a date with me after all. Not when she had her friends cockblocking me at the same time.

Naomi said nothing but watched me intently as I crossed my legs and glanced around. She had her arms crossed over her chest and I could feel her eyes boring into me. I had a feeling that when Iris came out, Naomi wasn't going to give us any privacy. She didn't look like she trusted me in the least.

"Silas?" It was Iris' voice and it sounded like an accusation.

I dragged my gaze away from Naomi to find Iris standing at one of the doors with a clipboard in her hand and anger in her eyes.

"What are you doing here?" Her voice sizzled threateningly.

14

IRIS

I couldn't believe what was happening, that Silas was really there. It wasn't that I was surprised he'd been able to find me—our organization's address was everywhere. I just hadn't expected him to be *interested* in finding me. I wasn't sure what I was supposed to say to him.

"Silas Denton?" Naomi hissed, equally angrily.

He looked a little confused and on the defense. He stood up, buttoned his jacket and walked toward me. His voice was smooth, smooth enough to melt me directly into a puddle. "Can we talk?"

I gritted my teeth, trying not to burst into flames where I stood. We weren't at a fundraiser or a fancy party and yet Silas looked like a million dollars. He had a sharp tailored suit on, a dark power tie, his hair was perfectly in place, and he looked like he'd just stepped out of a fashion ad.

"I don't think there's anything we have to talk about," I said, trying to remain calm.

Naomi was glaring at him too, and if I were him, I would have walked away right then. But he didn't. "Okay, I know I have things to apologize for, but I would like to do that in private. Do you have an office we can go to?"

"No, I don't have an office we can go to and I certainly do not need you to apologize to me for anything," I snapped.

Silas glanced at Naomi frustratedly before he looked at me again. "Okay, let's step out then."

"I don't think you're hearing me," I said, walking toward him. I was filled with rage. I felt used and defiled. Who did he think I was? How stupid did he take me to be? Did he really think he could seduce me into washing his family's sins away? "We have nothing to discuss."

Silas stared confidently back at me. His blue eyes were darkened and heavy. He was not going to scare easy, but what else could I expect from a man like him anyway?

"Iris, I know I've offended you, and I would like to apologize to you for my behavior last night. I shouldn't have reacted that way to your daughter."

I crossed my brows. That was what he thought my aggression was about? He came to apologize to me about *that*? What did he think was going to happen after his apology? That I'd forgive him and fall right into his arms? That he could fool me into kissing him again? Did he seriously think I wouldn't recognize that name?

I shook my head. "This has nothing to do with my daughter, and everything to do with that check you gave me."

"You really shouldn't let your pride get in the way of accepting the money my family is generously donating to your organization, Iris," he growled.

I could sense his anger building up too. Neither of us were enjoying this situation now.

"My pride?" I hissed. "You think this is about my pride?"

Silas stared at me.

"This is more than just pride. This is about doing what is right. We don't want your tainted money, Silas *Denton*," I hissed pulling the check out of the back pocket of my jeans and holding it up.

Of course he'd figured out what I was talking about by that point. I ripped the check apart in two and dropped it to the ground.

Silas watched in silence. He pushed his hands into the pockets of his pants and stood silently by.

I glared at him. "Is there nothing you would like to say for yourself now?"

It wasn't just Naomi and myself who were in the room now. Sarah, a few other volunteers, and a handful of women we'd been counseling all came out of the rooms to see what the commotion was.

But Silas didn't look intimidated. Nothing fazed him. "What could I possibly say to you now that would change your mind? You've made your judgment already."

There was a part of me that wished it hadn't turned out the way it did. I hadn't planned on it being a public humiliation for Silas. In fact, I hadn't planned on ever seeing him again or ever saying those words to him. I was carrying that check around with me because I just wanted to get rid of it.

"How could you attend that fundraiser? How could you deceive me that way and hand me a check? Expecting us to fall for all of it after everything your family has been involved in, in this neighborhood?" My voice was strained.

I didn't know how to feel. I was capable of being angry with him when he wasn't standing right there in front of me. But with him there, seeing his handsome face and recalling the way he made me feel, it was difficult. I was hoping he would give me some kind of an explanation, even though I knew there wasn't one.

He took his hands from his pockets and pulled down on his jacket. "Let's be honest here, Iris. You're not really looking for my answers, are you? You've made up your mind already. Anything I say to you now is only going to add fuel to the fire. I think the best thing to do now would be for me to walk away."

I couldn't say anything more. Silas looked at each of us before walking toward the door.

"Have a nice night ladies," he said as he stepped out of the building.

Naomi turned to me, as did everyone else.

"What is going on here?" One of the volunteers spoke up, voicing everyone else's thoughts.

"Nothing. It's over. Let's just forget about this and move on." Sarah tried to calm the questions.

"But Iris just tore up a check from that man. What does that mean?" another volunteer asked.

All their voices were fading around me. I knew everyone was talking at the same time but I couldn't really hear their words. All I could think about was that Silas had behaved in a perfectly gentlemanly way, and even though I had every right to be angry, he didn't deserve to be treated that way.

15

SILAS

Fuck

I rushed back to my car, jumped in and drove off before I could look in any other direction. I knew the best thing to do for me right then was to just go and never look back. I'd been so caught up in trying to think of ways to apologize to Iris about her daughter, that I hadn't even considered the possibility that she might recognize my last name.

Running from the scene, I realized how stupid I had been.. If she was from southside, and more importantly, had been affected by drugs in some way in her life and was running an anti-drug organization there—it was obvious she had heard of the Denton family.

Why hadn't I thought of that before? Like when I was signing my name on that check!

Fuck.

I banged my hands into the steering wheel and shook my hair out. I should have pre-empted it. I shouldn't have gone to see her again. I should have just accepted the fact that Iris and I were not going to work out and I should have let sleeping dogs lie.

Instead, I had just walked into an anti-drug charitable organization in the old neighborhood that the family operated out of. I had to face a room full of people who hated me and I had just knowingly humiliated myself.

The rage for my father resurfaced all over again. I was tempted. I was so tempted to just drive over to his new fucking house, to storm through the front door and tell him in great detail every way in which he'd destroyed my life and ruined our family. The only person to blame in all it was him. Charles Denton.

But I didn't drive to his house, instead, I drove all the way to the downtown docks and parked my car. I just needed some space to breathe.

I was seething mad still. I got out of the car and walked to the edge of the docks. There were yachts parked out there, a few of them were even having parties and music was playing loudly. I stayed away from them, remaining in the shadows, pacing and thinking.

I could just leave, the way Alex and Miles did. The way Sadie was traveling around the world. Why was I the idiot who stayed? Why did I feel sorry for our father? He was the one who dug himself his own grave and alienated his family.

I knew he blamed himself for Mom's death, and I knew he was right. I knew I was going to have bad days when I would feel like I still hadn't been able to get away, but it was beginning to get harder and harder. Even though we were not in the Southside anymore, and even though we'd made a drastic change in our lives and our family's circumstances —had things really changed that much?

Iris had mentioned 'tainted' money. Was all the money

we had really tainted? Would we ever be able to wash it off? Were Alex and Miles ever going to be able to run away from the legacy we were a part of?

I stood staring out at the dark waters in the night. The sun had set, there was a chill in the air and my hair was ruffled. For some reason, despite the things she had said to me and the way in which she'd humiliated me in front of those people—I didn't hate Iris. I got where she was coming from.

I shouldn't have listened to my Dad. I shouldn't have taken that check to the fundraiser. We should have just made an anonymous donation to the cause if Dad really wanted to make himself feel good about it, because it was never going to work.

It was an insult to hand that money over to Iris. My father, the work he'd done, was a huge part of the problem that Iris and her team were trying to solve. By giving her that money, we were trying to make it seem like money could solve the problem. Like it was easy.

I hated myself.

I wished she would have just let me speak to her in private so I could have explained. I owed her an apology for her daughter, and now I owed her an apology for trying to buy her off, too. I just wasn't getting it right with her, even though I really wanted to. There was something about her that made me crazy.

I stayed at the docks for a while longer, trying to unsuccessfully clear my head. When I got back in my car, I wasn't feeling any better. I didn't know what I could do to make it go away. Usually a shit ton of booze and banging some chicks helped, but that was not the solution tonight needed. I couldn't even think about another woman. Iris was the only one on my mind despite the fact that she despised me.

I drove slowly back to my apartment. There was nothing else for me to do at that point. I still had a company to run, a father to please, and a family to... chase down but never pull back together. I literally had nothing in my life to look forward to.

16

IRIS

Working late that night just felt impossible. The thing with Silas still rang loudly in my head. Instead, I picked Bess up early from the daycare and we walked home hand in hand. She kept me distracted for a while, talking about school and all the fun stuff she got to do that day. But everything that happened with Silas was still blaring so loudly in my brain it was hard to concentrate on Bess.

We went up to the apartment where I convinced Bess to take a quick shower while I made mac and cheese for dinner. She claimed she'd completed all her homework at the daycare and I trusted her because my daughter never lied, or at least I hoped she didn't.

While Bess was in the bathroom, I cooked. As I stirred the noodles in the bowling water, my mind drifted. Visions of Silas Denton and those deep blue eyes flashed in and out. I was confused.

I was beyond furious with the man. I was angry with *myself* for falling for his antics, for allowing myself to be thrilled and seduced by him. I was angry for nearly kissing him and of course for accepting that check.

And then he had the audacity to come find me at the agency. How stupid did he think I was?

At the same time, I couldn't help but feel guilty about the way I dealt with the situation. He wasn't being aggressive, nor was he being nasty or rude. He'd offered us money, which I should have simply declined and then parted ways. Instead, I'd participated in a public humiliation.

I didn't stop Naomi when she snapped at him. I didn't send the others away when they all crowded in the waiting room around us. I should have taken Silas aside to a room to talk in private, or we should have stepped outside and discussed the situation calmly.

This was exactly the kind of behavior that I warned people against—the women who came to our agency for help. *Do not act on impulse. Be kind to yourself and others. Forgive, let go, and move on. Be at peace.*

I had trained myself in those traits over the years, despite everything that had happened to me. Forgiveness and acceptance were the only ways forward, without which we could never be at peace with ourselves. I knew this philosophy greatly helped those who were trying to get over their drug addiction too.

Then why hadn't I been able to forgive Silas? Why had I reacted so potently toward him?

I stood over the pan while the creamy cheese sauce cooked searching for anything that justified my actions but I couldn't find an answer. By behaving that poorly with him, I had stooped just as low as him and his family's deeds. I should have risen above all that.

I didn't need to rip that check. I didn't need to throw it to the floor and make a big scene. Why did I feel like I had been personally betrayed by him when I didn't even know him at all.

"Mommy?" Bess' small voice interrupted my thoughts.

I blinked rapidly to get them out of my head before turning around to face her. "Have a seat sweetheart, dinner will be ready in just a few minutes."

I could sense Bess watching me work. She was extremely perceptive and I was sure she had detected the change in my mood.

"Are you sad, Mommy?" She eventually asked as I served the mac and cheese in two bowls.

"Sad? No baby, I'm just a little busy at work that's all." I tried smiling as I spoke, just to reassure her, but Bess wasn't falling for it that easily.

She batted her beautiful eyelashes as she picked up her fork. "But you said you were happy with the money we collected yesterday. You said it was going to help everyone."

I sat down across from her, pouring water into our glasses. Bess was pouting and wouldn't touch her food. It wasn't an exaggeration to say that nobody knew me like my daughter did. She could see right through me.

"I am happy about that, it's amazing, we're going to be able to do so much good work. It's just something else that's bothering me sweetie, but you don't have to bother yourself with that, okay?"

I started eating just to encourage her to eat too, but Bess continued to watch me intently. "What is it, Mommy?"

I sighed and looked up at her. "It's just this thing...I was rude to somebody. I had every reason to be, he deserved it..."

"But you said we should always forgive our enemies," Bess interrupted me.

I licked my lips. Was that what Silas was to me? Was he

my enemy? The cold hard truth was that he *was* my enemy in a way. He and his family stood for everything I was fighting against.

I nodded at Bess. "Yes, you're right. I should have forgiven him and stepped away, tried to stay calm."

Finally, she started eating too.

"Are you going to say sorry to him?" she asked after a few moments of silence.

"What?" The thought hadn't even occurred to me before that moment.

"But that's what you always say, Mommy, that we should say sorry to the people we hurt, no matter how difficult it is for us to say it."

I watched Bess, her big green eyes were staring up at me expectantly. She was right, she was right about everything. As proud as I was of her for knowing to do the right thing, I wished she wasn't right in that situation.

I chewed on my lip and took in a deep breath. "I don't know honey, I know that would be the right thing to do but I'm not sure I can actually do it."

Bess ate more of her dinner and smiled. "I know you can do it, Mommy, I believe in you."

I smiled back at her. If only things were that easy. But talking to her had made me feel better somehow and I was grateful to her for that.

17

SILAS

Sitting in my office, I groaned listening to the conversation going on and on. It was the new contractors we were trying to come to an agreement with for the new project. Lena was standing behind me making notes while our conversation carried on.

It had been a busy morning and it was only going to get busier through the day. That was good. Being immersed in work like that meant that I didn't have to think about Iris or my family and the Southside.

So, when the receptionist buzzed in to tell us there was a Ms. Iris Neilson in the lobby there to see me, I really had no idea what to expect. Was it some kind of a joke?

Lena obviously had no clue what was going on and she was about to tell the receptionist that I was too busy to deal with random people looking for a meeting.

"No, I'll see her," I snapped, interrupting the conference call.

Lena looked at me in surprise and I turned to the speaker phone again. "I'm sorry gentlemen, but we'll have to cut this meeting short today. I'll have my assistant contact you with another suitable date and time to continue this discussion."

I could sense the men on the other end were taken aback. We were so close to finally coming to an agreement on this, but it didn't seem like it was going to happen that day and I was tired of listening to them. I ended the call before they could say anything more.

I looked up at Lena who was still standing there with all the files in her arms. "Mr. Denton..."

I shook my head. "Yes, I'm fully aware I have another conference call in twenty minutes. I'm hoping my meeting with Ms. Neilson won't spill into that."

"Is this something I should add to your calendar for the day?" Lena continued, picking up a pen to scribble into her notebook.

"No, it's fine. It's a personal matter. You can go now." Just as I said that, there was a knock on the door.

"Come in!" I called out.

The receptionist had led Iris up to my office and they were standing at the door. Lena glanced at me one more time. I was aware that she was under the impression she knew every detail about my life, but she would be wrong. I nodded at her and she left the room, grazing past Iris on her way out.

The receptionist pulled the door shut as Iris stepped in. She looked abashedly around my office. Her cheeks were flushed pink, her green eyes were bright and sparkling with curiosity. I watched her in silence for a few seconds. She was silent too. Maybe she was trying to think of what to say as well, but I was in shock. I wasn't expecting to see her again, especially not like that.

Unlike the fundraiser, she was dressed way more casually. She was in a pair of tight fitting jeans and a blouse with a long, thick, aztec designed sweater over top. Her dark hair was straight and not as neat as the last time I had seen her. She had very little makeup on but still looked fresh and beautiful.

"Thanks for seeing me on such short notice," she said to me.

We were standing some distance away from each other. It seemed like neither of us wanted to close the gap. For the first time, she actually looked nervous as she spoke to me.

"What are you doing here, Iris? I didn't expect to see you again," I replied in a somber voice.

She didn't know how excited I was to see her. Things were constrained between us. As far as I knew, she hated me with a vengeance. Was her appearance at my office about the check she'd torn up? Had she changed her mind?

I saw her gulp and then look down at her feet nervously. "I know. I didn't think I could actually do this either. Face you again, I mean, but I just..."

I interrupted her. I could see how difficult this was for her and I wanted to make it easier. "Do you want me to write up another check for you?"

She looked up at me, her eyes wide with anger. Once again, I'd offended her. "That is not why I'm here. It's not about the money."

I stepped from behind my desk and proceeded toward her slowly, giving her enough opportunity to get away from me, back away to the door if she wanted, but Iris didn't make a move.

"It's okay if you've changed your mind about the check, Iris. I understand. It was a lot of money."

She gritted her teeth and pushed her chin up in the air. Her nostrils were flared with anger and she shook her head. "No. I don't want you to write me another check."

That was hard for me to believe. If it wasn't about the check, what else could it be? How stupid did she think I was?

"Okay, I'm listening, what is it then?" I challenged her, coming to a stop right in front of her.

I had my hands in the pockets of my pants. Iris was staring up at me with her eyes widened. Her breasts were heaving while she tried to catch a breath.

I was waiting for an answer.

She gulped again and looked down at her feet, hanging her head like she was ashamed. I was prepared to hear the words...*yes, sorry, I want the check*. But those words never materialized. Instead, Iris looked up at me again and her lips trembled a little as she spoke.

"I just came here to say that I was sorry for the way I acted when you came to the agency. I was angry and I lost my temper. Even though we can never be friends, I would like you to accept my apology for my behavior, and for the way I embarrassed you."

18

IRIS

*E*ven as I stood there in front of Silas, I knew I'd made the wrong decision by going there. I should have just stayed away. I didn't owe him an apology. It was over between us. I'd insulted him enough to keep him out of my life forever. I'd made that very clear to him already, and yet, I was standing there in front of him... waiting for him to reply.

Apologizing to someone had never felt that difficult before, especially because of the way Silas was staring at me. My apology to him seemed more like an insult. He wasn't expecting it and he couldn't look away from me.

I should have stepped away from him, I should have put some distance between us but it was like my feet were frozen to the ground. Like we were stuck together.

"Did you hear me?" I eventually asked. I'd lost track of time, how long had we just been standing there staring at each other?

"Yes, I heard you, Iris. I just wasn't expecting an apology from you, that's all."

I nodded and licked my lips.

"So, this is not about the check?" He asked.

He still couldn't get that out of his head. He just couldn't grasp the fact that I could possibly go there for anything other than money. "I just came here to apologize. I did something horrible. Nobody deserves a public humiliation like that, especially not when you weren't doing anything bad."

"So, what you're saying is that you and your agency are going to forgive my family and me for everything we were involved in?" he asked.

I arched my brows at him. "Of course not!" I crossed my arms over my breasts. "One thing has nothing to do with the other."

Silas narrowed his eyes at me.

"I'm apologizing to you for my bad behavior. It does not mean that I, or the neighborhood, or the hundreds and thousands of people who were, and are still affected by your family business—can forgive you."

Silas clenched his jaw. He wasn't happy with that response, but I wasn't there to please him.

"So what are you doing here?" He growled.

I was beginning to feel an irritation creeping up on me. "I don't think you understand. I came here to apologize to you for causing a public scene in front of other people when I should have just politely sent you away."

"And you're not here because you want to make peace?" he asked, looking genuinely confused.

I was starkly aware of the fact that Silas had taken another wide step toward me. Our bodies were even closer to each other than before. I could smell his cologne wafting from his smooth skin. I could feel the warmth and strength of his body not too far from my grasp. Suddenly, I was very aware of the fact that I was in his space, that we could be touching any moment, and still, I wasn't pulling away from him.

"I don't think I have the authority to call for peace. I'm just trying to help people in my neighborhood. I'm nobody," I insisted.

"And yet, you thought you owed me an apology because you think I deserve it." I nodded, feeling my words sticking to my throat.

Silas' eyes were roaming all over me, taking in my body, the rise and fall of my breasts, and the way my lips were parted. The words being exchanged did not match the way we were looking at each other, like we were ready to devour one another.

Silas leaned forward toward me. When I saw his hand reach out for my face, I stayed perfectly still. Slowly and softly he pinched my cheeks with his thumbs.

"So, you did all this, you came here today just because you're a good person?" he asked.

Despite his fingers on my cheeks in a strange show of closeness, I held his gaze strongly. "You can call it what you will. It's one of my philosophies in life, something I teach my daughter and I try to follow in my own life."

I'd assumed that a mention of my daughter would freak him out again, but it didn't seem to make any difference. Silas continued to glare at me, and his hand dropped slowly from my cheek.

His other hand lifted up and rested on my hip. I couldn't move. I couldn't understand why my body was reacting that way to his touch, like I had no control over my own limbs.

"I don't understand why you're here, Iris..." he hissed softly.

"I just explained..." His mouth covered mine and I gasped.

He was gentle toward me at first, giving me a chance to push him away, but I didn't. I wanted him. Every cell in my body was screaming for him, and instead of stepping away, I moved toward him, pressing my hips to his body, feeling the power of his chest squeeze against my breasts.

Our mouths were tangled together, his tongue slipped into mine, and I welcomed him in.

His hands were all over me. He was peeling off my sweater while I untied his tie with a manic obsession. He was using his body to push me backward until I pressed against the wall. I kissed him back hungrily. Nothing else mattered in that moment, just his hands on me, his mouth heated against mine.

His hands inched up beneath my blouse, cupping my breasts while our mouths moved together. I could feel the throbbing of his cock in his pants pressed against my thigh. He was big. I unzipped him and quickly took him in my hand. He pinched and squeezed my nipples under my blouse and I squealed with pleasure.

Our mouths parted and his tongue traveled down my neck as I fluidly stroked his cock. He was already so hard for me, just like how wet I could feel my pussy was for him.

As much as I tried, I couldn't stop myself. I didn't want to stop.

A buzzer went off on his desk, interrupting us with a jolt. It was like a slap in the face and I pushed against him. Silas stepped back from me immediately.

His tie was undone, his pants were undone too and I could see the bulge of his cock. His usually neat slick dark hair was ruffled and out of place.

I was out of breath, in shock and I couldn't look at him. I tried to smooth my clothes and settle my hair while he walked back to his desk and answered the call on the intercom.

"Mr. Denton, your two o' clock conference call is ready to be dialed in." It was a woman's voice, most likely the blonde who was in his office earlier and didn't fail to glare at him.

"Just give me a few minutes, Lena," Silas growled before ending the call.

Both of his hands were on his desk and his back was turned to me. I didn't have a mirror to check my makeup but I was pretty sure it was all a complete mess. How was I supposed to leave his office looking like that?

"I should go," I said meekly.

Silas ran a hand through his hair and slowly turned to look at me. His eyes were heavy. He looked like a man who regretted his actions. How was I going to forget how his cock had felt in my hand?

"Yeah, you should," he finally replied.

Okay, so we weren't going to talk about what just happened? Maybe we didn't need to talk about it at all because it happened to him all the time. Did he do it with that blonde too? His assistant, or whoever she was? I was horrified with myself. I was actually beginning to sound jealous.

I tried to quickly gather myself and I turned to walk to the door.

"Iris!" His voice was strong and sturdy.

I stopped in my tracks.

"Tell me again why you came to my office?" he asked.

A devilish grin was tugging the corner of his mouth and

it made me feel sick. Was he seriously implying I came to see him today because I wanted *that*?

"Fuck you, Silas Denton," I said and I strode to the door, opened it with a snap, and slammed it behind me.

The blonde from earlier was standing right outside with some files in her arms. Had she been trying to listen in? She took one long look at me while I glared back at her and I was certain she knew what was going on. My hair and my makeup in disarray would have given it all away.

"Have a nice day, Ms. Neilson," she said, in a polite professional tone I just barged past her, feeling even more furious than before.

I kept my head down as I rushed through the corridor to the elevator. I tried to recall my way there but I kept taking the wrong turns so it took me even longer to get to the elevator.

When I did eventually get in and was alone in there, I felt relieved. That was not at ALL how I meant for that to go.

I was okay as I rode the elevator down. I was okay as I walked through the lobby of the building and into the parking garage. But as soon as I got in the car I was panicking all over again. I hadn't even driven out of the parking lot yet. I was too miserable to move.

Why did I let Bess guilt-trip me into that?

She was right, it was my policy to never behave rudely to anyone, no matter how much I believed they deserved it—but I shouldn't have come to his office to apologize to him.

He didn't deserve that either.

I tried to but I couldn't wipe the image of that smirk from my head. How proud he looked when he asked me if I'd come to see him because I was looking for a booty call made me sick.

Argh!

That was not who I was. I didn't make stupid spur of the moment decisions like that. I should have never allowed Silas to get so close to me, to touch my face like that, to kiss me. But that body. That cock. That mouth on me! Nothing had ever felt so good before. No other man had made my body react to him like that. Silas was definitely very good. He knew exactly how to make a woman feel like she was on top of the world.

I started my car, just so I could do something other than sit there. Putting the car in drive, I slowly pulled out of the parking garage and out onto the street. I had to get back to work at the café. No matter how he treated me, I still had a job to do, and money to make for my family.

I checked myself in the rearview mirror as I drove. I would have to give my hair a comb and touch up my makeup before I walked back into the café again. Would I even be able to face my colleagues? What if I had to face Bess or Naomi, would I be able to make eye contact with them?

I still hadn't decided when exactly I was going to come clean to Naomi, who was my dearest friend, about what had been happening with Silas.

I felt so guilty. I could still feel his arms all over me. I could feel the sticky wetness of his tongue on my neck. I still wanted him despite everything he did!

I drove through traffic, trying to just calm myself, to prepare myself for facing people at work, but nothing was working. Silas had taken space in my head and he was not letting me eject him out. A part of me despised my actions while the other part of me wanted to be back in that gorgeous office with him, his hands all over me, feeling like nothing else mattered in the world but him.

When I arrived at the cafe, I parked in the lot and sat in my car for just a little bit longer.

What possessed me to walk into the Denton office building? Was I in my right mind when I thought I owed them anything? Maybe Silas was right after all, maybe I did have an ulterior motive for visiting him in his office, no matter how badly I wanted to deny it.

19

SILAS

I tried to focus on the conference call Lena set up, but nothing was making sense. My head was somewhere else. I was barely saying a word to the people on the call and I knew it was tanking big time.

Eventually, I had to cut that call short too and I asked Lena to just leave me alone in my office for a little while and clear my schedule for the next few hours. I could tell she was bubbling with a million questions, but she knew better than to ask me what was going on.

Iris had taken me by surprise.

Not only was I not expecting her to show up at my office, I wasn't expecting us to kiss, for her hand to be on my cock. None of it.

Not that I was complaining, but what the fuck was that?

I could feel my cock hardening just thinking about it.

I knew I had to find a way to distract myself.

So, I jumped out my chair and rushed from my office. I zoomed past Lena before she had a chance to say anything, and I headed straight for my dad's office. His secretary tried to stop me, saying that he was still taking his lunch and he didn't like to be disturbed, but I didn't give a shit.

I stormed into his office without knocking and he looked up from his desk in surprise. He had a big full tray of food in front of him and a napkin tucked into his collar.

"Hello, son," he said, dabbing the napkin on the corners of his mouth.

I banged the door shut behind me.

"We need to talk," I growled taking long strides in his direction.

"Okay, about what? You should have made an appointment with my girl. I'm sure we can fit you in some time later this evening."

I pulled out the leather chair across from him and sat down with a thump. "We need to talk now."

Dad sighed, pulling the napkin out of his collar and dropping it on top of his food. He'd barely made a dent in his lunch. The rest of it was going to go to waste. He hadn't yet given up most of his bad habits.

"What is this about, Silas? You look like you're going to burst a vein," he said.

"I didn't tell you what happened with the anti-drug organization, the check you made me drop off. I decided not to tell you because I figured I'd spare your feelings." There was a coarseness in my voice which he obviously recognized.

"Oh please, son, you don't need to spare my feelings. You can go right ahead and tell me what's going on," he said and crossed his arms on the desk.

"Well, the woman I gave the check to, tore it up in front of my eyes."

I knew he heard it because his eyes narrowed, but he raised his brow and tilted his ear toward me anyway. "I'm sorry, did you say she tore up a check for two hundred-thousand dollars? Is it because they're rolling around in cash?"

There was a tone of humor in his voice. For some reason, my father thought this was funny.

I didn't think it was funny in the least. "It's because they have no interest in accepting our tainted earnings."

Immediately his eyes darkened a bit. "Tainted earnings? Is that what she said?"

"I shouldn't have attended that fundraiser, Dad. It wasn't right for me to go. I shouldn't have made the offer to her." I rubbed a hand over my face while my father glared at me.

He took a deep breath and shrugged. "You offered them money at a fundraiser. That is the purpose of a fundraiser. Our family wanted to make a donation."

"What for, Dad? To right every wrong we've done in that neighborhood?" I snapped.

He rolled his eyes, dismissing my comment. "Because we have the money to spare and they are a charity looking for cash."

"You keep saying that like they're just some ordinary organization with no connection to us. Who the fuck are you kidding, Dad?" I stood up from my chair and he followed me with his intense gaze.

"What are you trying to tell me?" He lifted up from his chair, leaning forward on his desk.

I pointed at him, not backing down to his intimidation. "That you wanted me, the scapegoat of this fucking family, to go to that fundraiser and make that donation because you feel guilty and because you think that somehow, this money is going to help you sleep better at night."

He was taken aback, rarely being spoken to like that, especially not by me. I watched as my father steepled his fingers and drew in a deep breath. "So, what do you want me to do about it, Silas?"

I stood up and jammed my finger into the top of the desk. "We should have kept that donation anonymous. If you really want to make a fucking change, do something meaningful for that agency and don't beat your drums while you're at it. The last thing you should be expecting right now is praise and acceptance."

I didn't wait to hear what he had to say to that. I turned and stormed back out of his office. Maybe the people outside had heard me raging at him and were shocked by my behavior but I no longer gave a damn. What was I supposed to say anyway? He kept everything so secret from the public. I couldn't tell them my father was a criminal. That his sins had bloodied my hands too.

I walked back to my office and locked the door behind me so Lena couldn't drop in unannounced.

Meeting Iris, hearing her speak, everything about her—had stirred up new emotions in me that I had no control over. Why did I suddenly want to solve this? Why couldn't I just brush it under the carpet like I'd always done? That was what our family was good at.

20

IRIS

It was another night of me cooking dinner while Bess was in the bathroom taking a quick shower. I'd somehow managed to get through work at the café, and then the agency, and still get home early. After the day I had, all I really wanted to do was slip into bed and go to sleep. I was emotionally and physically exhausted and felt like I was going to pass out.

As much as I wanted to tell Naomi what was happening in my life, I hadn't been able to face her. I was still so guilty. Too guilty to even look at Bess when she spoke to me.

I was making a quick bean casserole for dinner and wished I'd bought myself a bottle of wine on the way home. If there was ever a night I needed a drink, that would have to be it. I opened the cupboards in the kitchen, looking for any remaining drop of alcohol, when I heard a knock on the front door. I wasn't expecting anyone, but sometimes Naomi liked to drop by for a surprise visit, so I thought it was her.

I turned the burner down, wiped my hands on a dishcloth, and went up to the door swinging it open. It wasn't

Naomi on the other side, it was Silas, and he had a huge bouquet of red roses in his hands.

"I hope I'm not intruding," he said.

I was too shocked to say anything for the first few moments. "H...how did you know where I live?"

Silas was grinning. "It's not very hard to find out where the famous and beloved Iris Neilson lives in this neighborhood. All I had to do was ask a few locals."

I hadn't invited him in but Silas stepped into the apartment anyway. "Something smells good, cooking dinner?"

He was looking around, casually, like nothing out of the ordinary was going on, like he just stopped by all the time. I left the front door open because I didn't want him getting any wrong ideas.

"I think you should leave, right now. My daughter is in the house. We're about to have dinner. I can't believe you would just march up here without a call or anything!"

He glanced at me but didn't seem to notice, or care, that I was angry. "That's good, I'll finally get to meet her,"

Why was he acting so tone deaf? "*Finally?* Just a few days ago you didn't even want to see me again because I have a daughter!"

He looked over at me with a seriousness to his face that I wasn't used to as he shook his head. "I overreacted. I shouldn't have behaved that way. I want you to accept my apology for acting like a complete dick. I seriously have nothing against kids."

I stepped up toward him, hoping he'd be able to see the anger in my eyes. "I don't think you're hearing what I'm saying. I want you to leave because I don't want you in my house!"

"Hello." It was Bess.

She was in the living room, all freshly changed into her

pajamas and with her hair damp from the shower. Silas turned to her, and before I could say anything, he rushed over to her, bending down on one knee. "Hello, these flowers are for you. I'm Silas."

He extended the bouquet to my daughter who accepted it from him graciously and with a smile.

"I'm Bess," she said and they shook hands like they were both adults.

"It's lovely to finally meet you. Your mom and I are friends and she can't stop talking about you," he said, which was a little bit of a lie but it made Bess smile.

She looked at me with that all too familiar look in her eye, the one she got when she liked someone. I knew it wasn't her fault. At first glance, there was very little to not like about Silas Denton. "Mommy, will Silas be having dinner with us? Where should I put this?"

I went up and took the bouquet from her. We had just one vase in the house which was rarely used.

"Excuse me," I murmured, feeling overwhelmed as I disappeared into the kitchen for a few moments to fill up the vase with water.

I brought the bouquet back to put the vase on the coffee table by the couch and found Silas and Bess talking. She was telling him about school and her friends, and Silas sounded interested, asking her questions. He was really selling himself to her for some reason. Why? What was he hoping to gain?

"Okay, it's dinner time," I said, interrupting them.

"I'll set you a place," Bess declared with glee but I wrapped my arms around her to stop her from going to the kitchen.

"Honey, I think you should say goodbye to Silas, I'm sure he has other engagements for dinner."

"But he said he would have dinner with us," Bess looked up at me with a pout.

I glared at Silas who was smiling. He knew very well that I couldn't push him out of my apartment after that.

"I'm not sure we have enough..." I tried to protest but Bess had already wriggled out of my arms and ran away to the kitchen.

"She's precious," he said.

I hooked my hands on my hips. "Are you seriously doing this right now? What part of, I don't want you in my house don't you get?"

Silas shrugged as he walked toward me, coming to a stop next to my shoulder. "I couldn't refuse a little girl's request. And who are you kidding, Iris? I can see the thirst for me in your eyes. You can't hide it, don't even try."

He walked past me into the kitchen, leaving me standing there in the living room, feeling light-headed and breathless.

I couldn't believe he'd actually spoken to me that way. In my own house! But he was right. Since he walked into my apartment, all I could think about was his body and his lips on mine.

I was so screwed.

21

SILAS

The food was good and the kitchen table was cozy. Sweet Bess was the only one doing all the talking because her mother seemed too afraid or uncomfortable to say anything.

Of course, I hadn't planned for this to happen. I hadn't come looking for her apartment because I wanted to gate-crash their family dinner, but instead I just went with the flow. I hadn't expected Bess to like me or welcome me but when she did and I couldn't refuse her hospitality.

Besides, watching Iris squirm in her seat was funny. I knew she was keeping an eye on me but avoided staring at me directly, which was comical and cute.

Bess was a big talker and a lot more mature for her age than I'd expected. All I had to do was ask her one small question and she could talk about it for the next fifteen minutes without stopping. In fact, she was the one who filled me in on a lot of the details of her mother's charitable agency. Iris had told me nothing.

It seemed like there couldn't possibly be a single dull

moment with Bess around. I ate heartily and then I tried to help Iris clear the table but she refused to accept my help.

"Bess, honey, it's time for bed. You should say goodnight and go to your room now," Iris finally said, interrupting something her daughter was saying.

"But Mommy..." Bess started to protest.

Iris was shaking her head. "Off to bed young lady. It's a school night, no excuses."

Bess was pouting, but she was obedient. She looked at me and I held out my hand to her and we shared another handshake. "It was lovely to meet you, thank you for the meal and I hope to see you soon again."

Bess nodded. "Good night, Silas. I hope to see you soon again too."

Then she smiled at her mother and Iris forced a smile onto her face. "Go ahead honey, I'll be there soon to tuck you in and read you a story. Brush your teeth."

Bess went rushing away and Iris and I were alone again, in the kitchen this time. She took her time to calm herself. She pushed the chairs back, wiped down the kitchen table with a damp towel, and made herself busy around the kitchen.

"Hey, Iris. Hey!" I said, trying to get her attention but she kept her gaze turned from me.

"What? What do you want to say? What more could you possibly have to say to me now?"

I tried to catch her eyes but she looked away from me.

"Okay, so you're saying this was a mistake? That when your daughter asked me to stay for dinner, I should have just walked out of the house?"

She finally looked at me, her face was pinched. She was still mad at me. "You shouldn't even have come here. You shouldn't have brought that bouquet. You didn't have to pretend to be nice to my kid!"

"Iris, I wasn't pretending," I said and stepped toward her.

She looked up at me with her brow crossed. "What do you want, Silas? I've made it very clear to you that I don't want anything from you."

"You're lying to me and you're lying to yourself." I stepped up closer, cornering her into the kitchen counter.

She could have slipped away if she wanted to, but I knew she didn't want to. "I shouldn't even be talking to you."

I was towering over her, I could feel the way her body was slowly beginning to shudder. I pictured lifting her up on the counter, her legs wrapped around me. I could push my hands up under her blouse right then, feel her tender full breasts in my palms.

"But here you are, talking to me," I whispered.

She leaned backward, just a few inches over the counter so she could look into my face. I could almost taste her, feel the sweetness of her mouth in mine. What was it about her that was driving me that crazy?

"There is absolutely nothing about you that I approve of. I want you to know that," she hissed.

The words were spewing out of her and yet, it seemed like she couldn't drag her body away from me.

"I know that. You despise me. If you could, you and your friends would destroy my family."

"Yes, we would," she hissed again.

She was searching my eyes, waiting for me to make my next move. To touch her. Her breasts were rising and falling with desire. All I wanted to do was wedge my hands between those delicious thighs and feel the heat of her pussy through her clothes.

But I stepped away.

"So, have dinner with me," I said.

Iris took a second to process that. She gulped then wrinkled her forehead. "What?"

"Have dinner with me. A meal you haven't cooked yourself. At a restaurant. I know the perfect one. Boheme, St. Claire Street." I was backing away from her, while Iris just stared at me like she couldn't comprehend my language. "Tomorrow, I'll book a table for eight o'clock, and I'll completely understand if you don't show up."

She was slowly starting to shake her head. I didn't want to wait to find out what she wanted to say. I turned and walked out of the kitchen, across the living room, and left her apartment. Thankfully, she hadn't followed me.

I climbed the stairs down to my car in a hurry. None of it was planned. I had no idea what I was doing.

I'd never asked a girl out on a date like that before. I didn't date. Especially dinner dates, where we couldn't go back to my place after just a drink or two.

A dinner would mean that we would actually have to sit down and talk, and there was no guarantee that she would even show up.

22

IRIS

I couldn't believe I was really getting ready to go on the date...the dinner with Silas.

I tried to put off my decision for as long as possible but by the time it was six, I knew I had to decide. If I was going on a date with Silas Denton, I would have to bring my A game.

Naomi agreed to babysit Bess for the night. I told her I had a business dinner with someone who could potentially be a donor. She knew how hard I was working to raise more money but when she showed up at the apartment and saw me in my dress for the night, she knew immediately that it was no ordinary dinner.

"Wow. Who on Earth is this potential donor?" she asked, following me into the apartment.

I turned to her, blushing, putting on my earrings. I wasn't sure what to wear to a place like Boheme. It wasn't the kind of restaurant that my daughter and I frequented. All I knew was that I would have to try my best to fit in at a place that wasn't made for me.

Since I didn't own many fancy pieces of clothing, the

fanciest of which I'd already worn to the fundraiser, I decided I just needed to keep it simple. I went with a little black dress, one that stuck forgivingly to my shape and had a deep square neck and slim sleeves. It wasn't too short, reaching just above my knees but I was aware of how it made my butt and breasts look. If Silas looked at me that way again, the way he had the night before in my kitchen, I knew I'd be dripping wet before I even sat down.

The only reason I couldn't resist going to Boheme was because of what he'd done to me the night before, how he'd withheld that kiss.

I straightened my hair and tied it in a sleek neat ponytail. I did my makeup the way I liked it best, neutral and nude with a little bit of shimmer. I didn't bother with high heels but the shoes I was wearing were sexy and appropriate.

Naomi was right, it wasn't exactly a business meeting attire. It was obvious I was trying to make an impression.

I smiled at my best friend and then gave her a twirl. "You like?"

She arched an eyebrow. "I like very much, and whoever you're meeting will like very much too. You have to tell me who it is though."

I licked my lips and stared at her, trying to weigh my options. If I told her about Silas right then, I wouldn't be able to make it to dinner on time. She'd want to know all the details.

"I'll tell you later, I promise," I said and lunged forward so I could give her a quick peck on the cheek.

She followed me to my bedroom, watching as I applied the finishing touches to my makeup and put on my perfume.

"Is this a date, Iris?" she asked me in a serious tone.

I saw her reflection in the mirror. She didn't seem mad, she had an excitable twinkle in her eye. I clamped my clutch shut after I'd slipped in my phone and some of the makeup I'd need. "I don't know what it is. I'm not sure why I'm even doing this, it feels wrong."

Naomi shook her head and walked toward me. "If this feels wrong because of Bess, then it really shouldn't. Honey, you need to get your own life, away from this neighborhood, and your work, and even your daughter sometimes. You've dedicated yourself to all this for long enough. Go and explore your other options. There is nothing wrong with that."

I gulped guiltily. If only she knew who I was seeing. She wouldn't be so understanding. Naomi knew how much anger I felt toward that family. But how was I supposed to describe to her the effect that Silas had on me?

"I think I'm just going to take this one night at a time for now. This isn't really going anywhere, but I just..."

"Just have fun!" She declared and gave me a hug.

I nodded. "I'll go check in on Bess. She's had her dinner, brushed her teeth and now she's reading a book in bed. She should be asleep in half an hour."

We both went over to Bess' room and I hugged and kissed her goodnight and told her I'd be back very soon. I had rarely ever spent time away from her, but she didn't seem uncomfortable with it.

"Maybe we can read that book together?" Naomi suggested, stroking Bess' hair.

I smiled at them and blew them a kiss before I left the room.

At the front door, I breathed in deeply, preparing myself for the night. Not only was it going to be my first 'date' in a very long time, it was a date with Silas. Did he even consider it to be a date?

Why else would he invite me to dinner?

Unless he thought that buying me dinner was a necessity before I slept with him?

Did I want to sleep with him? Yes. He was irresistible.

Was it a good idea to sleep with him? No. We would never be able to get past our differences.

So, why was I even going tonight?

It was too late to change my mind, so I had to go. My nerves were high, so I decided not to drive. The trip on the L was good, time to calm myself before making an entrance.

23

SILAS

There was no way Iris was showing up for dinner. If I was a betting man, I would have bet a lot of money on being stood up that night.

I arrived early at the restaurant and was led to the romantic table for two at the back. It was a fashionable upscale restaurant with a complicated menu. The lights were dim and the tables and chairs were all low and very comfortable. There was some slow acoustic music playing in the background and extravagant splashes of color everywhere. The light fixtures, the cushions on the chairs, the cutlery, all giving an eclectic eye appealing vibe.

It was obvious that a lot of thought and effort had gone into making the place seem young and sophisticated at the same time, and I was worried if Iris would feel comfortable here. If she even showed up, that was.

I looked down at my watch several times. Ten past eight...then twenty past eight... I had ordered a bottle of the finest red wine on the menu and sampled my first glass. Another ten minutes and I decided I would finish the bottle myself, order some appetizers and then leave.

I'd dug my own grave with the invitation. I should have known better than to ask Iris Neilson out for dinner. A woman who despised me.

But then she showed up.

I saw her walk into the restaurant, looking unbelievably elegant and sexier than hell. She was speaking to the hostess glancing up at me as the hostess led her to the back. I stood up in surprise. I couldn't believe she was actually there. I couldn't take my eyes off of her.

That black dress, the way it stretched over her breasts, her beautiful glowing face, her sexy walk with her hips swaying. Everything about Iris screamed sensual. I was awestruck but somehow, I managed to gather myself. I held a chair out for her and she sat down without a word.

"Give us a few minutes, thanks," I told the hostess, who nodded curtly and walked away.

I sat down, smoothening my jacket and tie.

"I was prepared to be stood up tonight," I said, pouring some of the wine into her glass.

Iris finally met my eyes. "I can't imagine this happens to you often. Being stood up."

I didn't reply. There was a menu on her side of the table which she quickly picked up. It seemed like she would do anything to avoid direct eye contact with me. Was she shy about something? Was she angry?

"What made you come?" I asked.

Her eyes flickered so fast across the menu I couldn't really believe she was reading anything on the page. "I guess I was curious, why a man like you would want to have dinner with a woman like me."

Iris looked up at me then and I held her gaze. "Isn't it obvious?"

"You want to sleep with me," she stated, in a matter of fact way.

I twirled the glass of wine and then took a sip. Iris was watching me, following my every move. She didn't seem pleased, her nose crinkled and her lip twitching as if she had tasted something sour.

I put my glass down and flicked some lint off the sleeve of my jacket. "That may be so, but it isn't why I invited you to have dinner with me."

Her nostrils flared. She didn't buy it. Iris looked away and back at the menu. I couldn't stop staring at her, studying every curve of her face. But it was time to get down to business.

I leaned in toward her and she shifted in her seat uncomfortably. She looked up again, finding my face now stout and serious. "I want to disclose a few crucial things to you about me, about my family and our past."

Iris sat back, flipping the menu shut. She looked confused. "Why?"

"Because I feel it's important that someone knows, and I would rather it be you." A few moments of silence passed between us.

I could see the contemplation on her face, her mind trying to full understand what I was saying. "I don't understand, why do you want to tell me about your life and your family?"

I shrugged. "Because, I'm tired of running from it, or hiding from it, and when you look at me, you see a monster. I wish that you wouldn't see me that way."

Iris' eyes softened. She was chewing on her bottom lip, trying to think maybe, trying to decide if she could trust me. "What do you want me to do with this information?"

I smirked. "I don't know if you'll be able to do anything

with what I tell you, Iris. It's not like you could put us in jail. You could go to the newspapers with it, sure, and I'll leave it up to you. I honestly don't care anymore."

"Hi, are we ready to order?" A waitress had shown up beside us while Iris and I were staring at each other.

She looked down at the menu, flipping it open again. "I honestly have no idea what any of this is. I'll have this one I guess."

The waitress seemed a little flustered but she took the order down nonetheless. "And how would you like it cooked?"

Iris just looked up, glaring at her and the waitress scribbled something else down.

"And for you Sir?" She turned to me and I could hear her cheeriness weakening.

"I'll have what she's having," I said.

I knew Iris was spunky but I didn't realize she had the ability to scare people that much. I liked it. It made my desire deepen even further.

She was staring at me again, weaving her fingers together while her eyes assessed me. "Okay, go ahead, I'm all ears, Silas. Tell me what you're here to say."

24

IRIS

To say I was curious to hear what Silas had to say would have been an understatement. I had no idea what to expect, and his reaction was definitely not what I was expecting. I thought the dinner was just going to be a ploy on his part to get into my pants, but he hadn't made a move yet and it felt like he had no intention of doing so, either.

I sat watching him, trying not to be distracted too much by his handsome face and his perfect bone structure. Those glittering dangerous blue eyes bore into me. He looked so sexy in his dark designer suit. His tie was a rich purple making his eyes look even brighter.

"I am sure there isn't much I can tell you about the family business that you don't know already. My dad got involved in the drug trade at a young age. He grew up in the Southside, that was his life, and he started dealing drugs because that was the only way he knew to survive."

He didn't break eye contact with me and the way he spoke made it seem like he wasn't interested in gaining my sympathy. Then what did he want exactly? What did he hope to achieve?

I nodded lightly. I knew bits of the story about Charles Denton already. "I know he grew up on the Southside and I knew he got involved in gangs early on.".

Silas poured himself some more wine and drank. "My dad had no interest in a family. He didn't plan on having kids or marrying, or settling down in any way. He was a free spirit, never took the drugs he sold, and he partied hard."

While he spoke about his father I could sense a certain level of respect for him. I had never personally met Charles Denton, but I doubted I would respect him even if I did.

The drugs he and his family business sold in my neighborhood were responsible for the high number of addicts we were trying to help. The Denton family was one of the sources of the problem we were facing.

"Okay…" I murmured.

Silas continued, glancing down in his glass of wine. "But then he met my mom. She was from Florida, visiting family on the Northside. She had no connection to my dad or his life. They happened to bump into each other on an ice skating rink, of all places, and he fell for her immediately. She was young and beautiful and innocent, and for some reason, she fell for him too."

Silas was speaking of his mother fondly. I could see it in his eyes. I knew nothing about Mrs. Denton, but I got the feeling now that something happened to her.

"Where is she?" I blurted catching his gaze.

His eyes had grown dark and hardened. "She died."

I knew it was rude to ask, but I did anyway. "How?"

"My father has committed a crime, more often than not, he made the wrong moral choices in life, but he loved her.

He loved our mother," he said, not yet answering my question.

Silas did not seem like the kind of man who cried easily, but I could see that he was emotional. He wasn't having an easy time talking about his mother. He drank more wine. "As hard as it is to believe, they were happy together. My mother knew so little about him. He kept her in the dark about what he was really involved with. He tried to keep all of us in the dark."

I could feel my heart wrenching as I watched him speak. I didn't want him to hurt and I wished I could do something to make the process easier for him.

"How many siblings do you have?" I asked him.

"Two brothers and a sister, I'm the oldest."

There was an interruption. The food had arrived. It was a fishy dish, squid and octopus maybe, with some vegetables and a dressing. I had no idea what I was about to eat but I didn't really care.

Silas didn't seem very interested in the food either.

"So, you had a happy childhood?" I asked him, hoping to lighten the mood a little.

He shrugged and drew in a deep breath. "I thought I did. We all assumed we were leading a fairly happy life. We had the biggest, most lavish house in the Southside, with twenty-four hour security and constant help around the house. He treated my mother like a Queen, giving her every luxury she could want. The only thing he asked for, was that she wouldn't ask him questions about his work."

For the first time, it was occurring to me that maybe Silas and the rest of his family were just as much of a victim of the whole thing as the rest of the neighborhood.

"And she never did?" I asked.

He glanced at me as he drank some more of his wine. "I

don't think she did for several years, at least not while we were still young. She loved him and she had a luxurious life and...maybe she wanted to keep things simple."

"And she had no idea the kind of business he was involved in? The violence and the drugs and the number of people he was getting hooked onto that stuff? The families he was affecting?" I was getting emotional too and Silas glared at me. Was that anger or disappointment I was seeing in his eyes?

"You don't know my father. He did everything he could to hide it from all of us. He made sure we went to schools away from the neighborhood. We always had guards with us wherever we went. We weren't allowed to mix with kids in the area. We had a cushy childhood, sure, but it wasn't a normal one. Maybe my mom started to feel lonely and that was when she began asking the questions."

"Did he tell her?" I asked.

I was interested to know, I felt invested in the story.

Silas looked at me and sighed. "My father wasn't going to tell her that easily. He'd spent several years protecting her, and us, from that information. He resisted it, and slowly we saw their relationship beginning to fall apart."

Silas was nervous. He played with his watch, smoothened his tie...I still had no idea why he wanted to talk to *me* about all of it. What was he going to gain?

"Where were you? How old were you?" I asked.

He cleared his throat. "I was just out of college. I got into a Business Graduate Program with a company in London. My dad had made sure we got the very best education. But even though I was in a different country, I could sense things weren't right at home."

Neither of us had touched our food, it was getting cold, and just as well.

"Was she upset? Depressed?" I asked.

He nodded. "Our mother suddenly realized that she was alienated from everyone; she and her family had no friends. Her husband kept her locked in an ivory tower, just to protect her from his truth. Just because he never wanted her to find out the truth about him. He was sure he would lose her. She would never be able to support what he did. She would be disgusted by all the money and the luxury we lived in."

Silas' hands were on the table and I was tempted to reach for them. It was not easy for him to talk about his mom. I didn't know the full story yet but I could sense that something bad had happened.

"But she did find out eventually," he snapped.

I was afraid to hear more, but he continued. "She paid the servants in the house to talk and she hired a private eye to follow my dad. She spent four months collecting all this information on him. Things she never knew about her husband, the love of her life, the man she trusted."

My throat had gone dry, I knew something bad was going to happen.

"Mom lost it. She called me in London, crying and distraught, speaking gibberish over the phone. I got on the first flight back to Chicago and I came home to find her drunk, lying on the carpet in their bedroom. Dad had no idea, he was working. When she sobered up, she told me everything, and finally things started to fall into place. Even though I'd never tried to find out the truth myself, I guess I always knew. I always had that feeling."

I couldn't help myself this time, I reached for his hand. I was surprised to find that he didn't pull his hand away. He was warm and strong and looking me in the eye.

"We confronted Dad together. He laughed in our faces at

first and then fought with us. He told Mom that he did all this for her, to make her happy and to give her everything. It wasn't true. He got into the business a long time before he met her."

I squeezed his hand and Silas sighed. "But that got to her, she couldn't deal with it."

He was taking his time to finish the rest of his thought now.

"A week later, I found her in a pool of her own blood. She'd cut her wrists."

I sat back, trying not to gasp, but my hand flew up to my mouth. "Silas, I'm so sorry. I really am. I really don't..."

Silas shook his head. "This has nothing to do with you, Iris. I'm not telling you this story to gain your sympathy. I just wanted you to know the truth about my family. My father has a lot of things he has to account for, but the rest of us—when I wrote you a check from the family, it was because we weren't involved in it."

I gulped, staring at him with wild eyes. I didn't know what to believe, what to think. Did he want my forgiveness? What did he want? "I'm not sure I can help you, Silas. Thank you for sharing your story, I'm sure it's been difficult for you, but I don't know what you want me to do with this information."

He nodded and stuck his fork in the plate of food in front of him. "Nothing. I guess I was just hoping you would hate me a little less."

He wasn't smiling but his voice had softened considerably.

"I don't hate you, of course not," I mumbled.

He smirked. "You don't have to worry about saying the appropriate thing. My mother died a long time ago, nearly twelve years ago. The family has seemed to move on from it, I think."

He was eating, but I couldn't. Not after that conversation. "Was that why your dad got out of the drug business? Left the Southside?

Silas was chewing slowly when he looked at me. "His business started failing very quickly after she died. He was angry, but also irreparably damaged. He had no interest in anything anymore, and I knew I had to do something. I moved back to the States a few years later and quit my job. I decided I would help salvage the family money to some extent. I wanted to make the business clean, for Mom's sake."

While I was watching Silas speak, I suddenly realized that he was the kind of man who wasn't afraid of anything. He wasn't afraid of humiliation, of losing, of danger. He'd already lost too much. I didn't know whether to be afraid of that or feel safe in his presence.

"You're not eating," he said, interrupting his own dialogue.

I looked down at my plate and shook my head.

"Yeah, this food is shit anyway," he added and dropped his cutlery on the plate and stood up.

25

SILAS

We walked out of Boheme without having eaten. I paid what was owed and Iris followed me out into the night.

"Do you need my jacket? Are you cold?" I asked her.

She shook her head. "No, thanks, I'm not cold."

We were walking away from the restaurant, I wasn't entirely sure where we were headed, but Iris didn't seem to mind. She wasn't asking me many questions since I told her the truth. Maybe she thought I needed some space.

It hadn't been easy to just tell someone every dark secret of my past. Especially someone like Iris—who I was trying to impress, hoping she saw something more in me than just the exterior.

I'd told her everything. She could see for herself how fucked up the rest of my family was, along with me. Whatever sliver of a chance I had of being with her was gone. And all because I wanted to get that heavy burden off my chest.

After we'd been silent for a while, I turned to glance at her. "Are you hungry? I'm sorry about back there. I should have picked a better restaurant."

She shrugged. "I could eat, in fact, if you're not fussy, we could go over to the food truck that's usually parked here around the corner. They make a mean burrito."

I smiled. I liked the sound of that.

Iris led the way and I followed.

I didn't do dates for starters, and I definitely didn't do dates like that!

We found the food truck easily and there was a long queue. Neither of us minded waiting. We stood in line together, glancing sheepishly at each other from time to time, making small talk about Mexican food in general. There was still so much left unspoken between us and I wasn't sure if she would give me a chance to explain. Maybe she'd had enough.

Finally, we got our orders in and we carried our burritos over to a bench at the edge of a deserted dark park. We sat on the two corners of the bench, with a large gap between us.

Iris wasn't the neatest eater and it was funny to see her eat so messily. The sauces got everywhere and I had to run back to the truck and get more napkins. But the mess made us laugh, and it looked like she was actually having a bit of fun.

I nodded as I got to the end of my burrito. "That was some seriously good food."

Iris was smiling too. She sighed and dabbed some more tissues on her mouth. "Things got a little serious back there, huh?"

I wiped my hands. "I just wanted to come clean. I knew I'd offended you with that money, and you have every right to be mad at me and the rest of us. I just wanted you to know that if my mom was here, she would have genuinely wanted to do this for your organization, and I gave you the check for her, not because my dad wanted me to."

It was the truth. That was what I wanted her to know.

Iris looked down at her lap and then nodded. "Okay, yeah, I believe you." There was a soft grin on her face. "I still don't understand why you told me all this, but I guess in a way I'm glad that you did."

"Not many people know this about me. I've spent too much time working and building my career to make any real friends. My siblings don't live close to me because they wanted to get away from our father. It's just all a mess," I said, running a hand through my hair.

I could sense her shifting toward me on the bench.

"Silas..." she said my name softly, but I couldn't stop talking.

It was all coming hurtling out of me. "And if I could do something to help her, my mom, to make her see how much she meant to the rest of us, maybe she would..."

"Silas!" This time she said my name more sternly and I turned my head to look at her. She put a hand on my knee and the touch was electric. "I don't know if there was anything you could have done to save her. I'm sure you tried your best, but she was disappointed and hurt and depressed. I'm sorry that you and your family had to go through this, but you should move on."

Her voice was so soft and sweet, it sank right into my body and I knew I wanted to kiss her but I couldn't. She wouldn't have wanted me to kiss her. Just because I'd told her the truth didn't mean it absolved me of all my sins.

"None of us will ever move on, least of all my father," I said. "He is never going to forgive himself for his past and what that did to his wife. My brothers and my sister will never know the full extent of the truth because I will keep it hidden from them for as long as I can, and there won't be many nights that I'll be able to sleep."

Iris searched my eyes. She'd been silent for a while. I had no idea what she was thinking, but I just wanted her to say something. I'd never felt that raw or exposed before, and I wanted to know if she still had something to say. Maybe I'd ruined everything already.

"Silas, I want to go home with you tonight," she said.

26

IRIS

I was surprised at myself for making that proposition. I'd never said those words to any man before, but somehow it had seemed natural with Silas. The fact was, I didn't want the night to end.

He'd opened up to me. I didn't know what reasons he had to do that, but I was grateful for it. For the first time, Silas seemed more human to me, and not just some sort of perfect looking hunk of meat who I had to hate.

There were shades of gray in him, parts of him that would be difficult for me to get past, but if he was telling me the truth then he was never a part of the problem. It was and always had been just Charles Denton.

I felt closer to him. I wanted him. I needed to know if whatever was between us was going to go anywhere. So, I said those unimaginable words; *I want to go home with you tonight*. Silas stood up. He led me to his Cadillac without a word and I got in.

I wasn't thinking about anything else, just him and me, alone. He didn't live too far from the restaurant and within twenty minutes we were in his fancy penthouse.

"Wow. Talk about ivory towers," I commented, walking over to the glass wall on one side of his den that overlooked the Chicago skyline.

The lights were dimmed in the room and I sensed him walking towards me. "This is our business now. Real estate."

"I know," I commented.

I felt his hands on my shoulders. He was standing directly behind me, towering over me with his massive muscular body. I could feel his powerful presence and it sent chills down my spine.

"I've been trying, Iris, for the past four years, I've been trying to do everything I can to run a clean family business. I convinced my father. I know I'm going to make this work."

I turned to face him, tipping my face up towards him. "Why do you care so much what I think?"

His hands were on my arms, grazing my skin. I tried not to be distracted by how warm and powerful that touch was. "I don't know. I guess I have this idea that if you forgive me, *us*, the family...that somehow it would make it all just a little bit better."

I shook my head. "I can't do that, Silas. I can't forgive you on behalf of all these people whose lives your family business has affected. People who are facing the consequences of it to this day."

I was peering into his deep blue eyes. He clenched his jaw and nodded. "Yes, I know, it's stupid of me. I don't know what I was thinking."

His hand moved up my arm and neck till he was clutching the side of my face, tilting my face up to his. My lips parted. I could feel my stomach tightening, the wetness growing between my legs.

"But I'm glad I told you anyway. I wanted you to know the truth about me," he said in a softer voice.

The sexual tension had been so heightened between us, that his softness was surprising.

Silas kissed me. It wasn't just any kiss, it was THE kiss. Our lips touched and I opened my mouth wide, allowing his tongue to slip in. He pushed against me gently so my back pressed against the glass wall behind me and he kept me pinned to it.

I wrapped my arms around his neck and our bodies pressed together. I could feel his cock against me. I'd felt the strength and size of that cock already and I wanted to feel it again. But I didn't want to take the first step this time. He was leading.

His hands traveled down my dress, unzipping it along the way so the straps fell away. I gasped as my bare skin touched the glass wall, but it felt good. Everything felt good with him.

His mouth was still on me, devouring me, and my panties were soaking wet. Slowly, he started pushing my dress down, out of the way, letting it fall to the floor at my feet. I stood there against the window in nothing but black panties.

He cupped my breasts, gently at first and then he squeezed them tightly.

"I would have done anything to feel these in my hands," he said.

I bit down on my lip, reaching for his cock. He put his hand over mine, glaring into my eyes. "No, you don't get to make me go crazy this time."

What did that mean? My mouth hung open while his hands explored the rest of my body. He caressed my stomach, felt the shape of my thighs and my butt and harshly pulled at my panties. I was afraid he would tear them but he rolled them gently down to my ankles.

Silas was fully dressed and after he took off my bra, I was completely naked. Was this another move on his part to prove how he was the powerful one? How he had complete control over me?

My nipples were burning hot, aching for his mouth and his touch. He leaned forward and covered the right one with his open mouth. I sighed, knocking my head back and weaving my fingers into his hair. He licked and sucked on my breast, while he squeezed the other nipple, teasing it gently with his fingers.

My pussy tingled with desire. I rolled my hips with need. When Silas was done teasing my breasts, he pulled away from me and looked into my eyes with a grin.

"Someone's getting impatient," he grunted.

Just his voice was enough to make me lose control. How could he do this to me? How was I so close to coming even though he'd barely done anything to me?

Then he touched me between my legs and I felt the warmth of his fingers, the length of the middle one slipping into my pussy. I gasped, the air burning in my lungs as I dug my nails into his arm.

He stroked my pussy, rubbing my swollen sticky clit with his thumb. My body was on fire. I couldn't stop my hips from rolling, yearning for his cock. But just as suddenly as he'd started, Silas stepped away from me.

I gasped, feeling his fingers leave my body. I was so close to coming!

I glared at him with my shoulders heaving, waiting for an explanation. He still had that grin on his face. Removing his tie, his jacket, his pants came off, then his shirt, and for the first time, I saw Silas Denton naked.

His body was strong and muscular. His torso was chiseled, his abs were well defined, and his stomach was flat. As he slipped his boxer briefs off, I bit my lips, staring at his big proud cock hanging hard between his muscular thighs.

My mouth watered at the sight of it.

"On your knees," he grunted.

There was authority in his voice and I did as I was told. I lowered down on my knees, watching as Silas moved forward, holding his hard cock in his hand. He grabbed the back of my head, tilting it up to see my face.

"Open up," he said.

I opened my mouth wide. He stood over me, rubbing his cock against my lips. I moaned, sticking out my tongue, practically begging for it. He pushed into my mouth, slowly, steadily, letting my tongue run the length of his salty shaft. My tongue swayed back and forth, feeling the girth fill my mouth and throat. I could barely hold back a choke he was so big.

I held on to his thighs while my head bobbed forward and back, his cock ramming in and out of my throat. I loved how much control he had over me. I loved how he was using me for his own pleasure.

Silas pulled his cock out of my mouth and I gasped again. Still holding me by the back of my head, he started tugging me up. Before I knew what he was going to do next, he whipped me around. He pressed me into the glass wall, my breasts squeezed up against it. I felt like I was floating, looking directly out at the city skyline. It was breathtaking!

I heard the sound of the condom packet tearing. Just the thought of what was going to happen next sent shivers down my spine.

In the next moment his hands were all over me. He was caressing my shape again, every curve of my body. When he reached my ass, he slapped it hard. I felt the tingle on my skin. I winced and thrust my butt out toward him. "Is that all you got?"

He was standing right behind me, his eyes dark and heavy. He looked like he was in a trance. I didn't know if he could even hear me.

He slapped my ass again and I bit down on my lip. There was pleasure in the pain. I stuck my butt out toward him again and he caught it with both hands. He parted my butt and I felt the length of his cock against me. He was rubbing up against me. I leaned further into the glass. The stark difference in temperatures between the glass and Silas' cock made my breasts hard and my nipples erect.

His hands moved around my waist, dipping down until his fingers found my clit. His cock slid into my pussy from behind. The pleasure was explosive. Nothing had ever felt like that before.

His hips bumped against me as his fingers ran circles around my clit. We moved in unison, our bodies pushing back and forth against each other.

I moaned with every thrust. He pushed hard, forcing himself deep inside me. His fingers had taken control. My clit was swollen and throbbing and I couldn't hold it back anymore.

My knees wobbled and I nearly fell forward when I came, but Silas held firm to my waist. He didn't stop thrusting, didn't stop moving. His deep feral grunts were so sexy.

As my body writhed and shook from orgasm, his cock swelled, growing harder until finally he came. I could feel his shaft pulsing as he released his seed. I bit down on my lip, letting out a wild moan, my body shuttering wildly.

Our orgasms ended, slowly, like a flickering candle...my body still tingling. I could still feel him deep inside me till finally, he started pulling himself out.

I turned around slowly after he stepped away from me. We were both breathing hard. I ran a hand through my hair realizing I'd been sweating.

Silas pulled off the condom and looked up at me with those deep trance-like eyes. "I should get you a towel."

I said nothing. I watched him walking out of the room, totally naked and I turned around to face the skyline again. I was shaking my head in disbelief.

Now that it was over, I felt like I hadn't thought things through. There were so many ways that it was wrong, but it still felt so right. I didn't know what to do or think anymore.

Silas returned with a pile of fluffy fresh towels. "I wasn't sure how many you'd need. Or you can take a shower too, if you like."

I pulled a towel out and started dabbing myself. "This is enough, thanks, I need to leave soon anyway."

He didn't respond, but I didn't expect him to.

27

SILAS

*I*ris and I didn't speak while we cleaned ourselves up and got dressed again. She said she had to leave soon and I knew I couldn't stop her since she had a six year old to go home to.

There was a lot I could have said to her, but I'd never had that kind of conversation before. Sex was always the end of my night. I was inexperienced in what was supposed to come next.

I could still feel the soft wetness of her delicious pussy, her perfect body. I wanted to weave my fingers into her hair and hold her close It had been an extraordinary night. I wished I could have expressed myself better, but all I did was watch her from the corner of my eye as she wiped herself down with my towel and then started putting on her clothes.

Most of the women I slept with tried to hang around after sex. They usually wanted to stay for a drink, or sleep over and do brunch the next day. I'd gotten into the habit of having to tip-toe around the chicks I banged. But Iris seemed like she couldn't get out of my apartment fast enough.

Maybe she thought everything was a big mistake. Maybe sleeping with me went against all her rules.

I didn't put on my tie or jacket and while she tidied herself up, I walked over to the bar in the den and made myself a drink.

"Nightcap before you leave?" I asked from where I was standing.

"Just some water will do, thanks," she replied.

I poured her a glass and carried it over to her. We had yet to acknowledge what happened between us, but it seemed like she didn't want to talk about it.

Iris smiled politely as she took the glass of water. I could see her makeup lighter and a little smudged, her hair wasn't in the ponytail anymore, and not as sleek as before.

"How is Bess doing?" I asked.

She nodded. "She's fine, she knows how to keep herself busy."

"She's a great kid," I said.

Iris sipped her water like we were in a business meeting. I had to say something. I'd shared too much about my life already, and now that we had sex, how could I just let her go without saying anything? It seemed hypocritical. Besides, I knew no other way of expressing to her that tonight was different. It was more than just a one-night stand.

"Thanks for hearing me out tonight, you didn't have to do that," I told her.

Her eyes were sparkling and bright, she smiled a little. "It's kind of what I do at the agency."

"Well, you're good at your job."

"But I definitely don't have sex with them afterward!" she exclaimed.

Even though it was awkwardly inappropriate, we both managed to smirk at each other anyway. I just wanted to grab her by her shoulders and shake her and tell her how amazing the sex was.

"I'm glad you made an exception with me," was all I managed to say.

Iris put the glass down on the coffee table and clasped her hands together. I could sense she'd hyped herself up now to say something critical.

"Silas, I just want you to know that you don't have to worry about me becoming emotionally hung-up on this. I know we felt a chemistry that night at the fundraiser, and we've got it out of our system now."

No other woman had sounded that level headed to me before. It literally felt like we were in a business meeting, and she was laying down her terms for a deal.

"And we can move on. I'm glad you shared your history with me, and I will gladly accept the check from you if you make it out from your mother and the rest of your family. I would prefer it if you could leave your father out of it. I will not deny your mother's wishes to right your father's wrongs."

I gulped. She had no idea how it felt to hear her say those words. Just because those wounds were from twelve years ago did not mean they'd healed completely.

I nodded. That was all I could do.

"I should go, Bess and Naomi will be worried. I never stay out this late."

A smile flickered on her face and then we walked to the front door.

"I should call you a cab," I said at the last minute.

Where were my manners? I wasn't thinking straight.

She shook her head. "It's okay, I can get one easily. You don't need to worry about it."

Iris stepped out, pressing the button to the elevator quickly as if she were trying to leave as quickly as possible.

"I'll mail you the check tomorrow," I said.

And those were the last words I said to her before she got in the elevator. I deeply regretted it.

I toyed with the idea of chasing after her, but she seemed like she just wanted to be left alone. I had to respect her wishes.

I was alone in my dark apartment, anxious, thinking about Iris and how amazing it would have been if she had stayed the night. I had never felt that way about a woman before.

28

IRIS

Naomi had fallen asleep on the couch with the TV. She was snuggled up under a light blanket with the remote in one hand and her phone in the other. I smiled at her, guilt bubbling in my gut. She had no clue what I'd been up to that night.

I checked in on Bess, then changed out of my dress and freshened up a little before putting on my pajamas, a stark contrast to the sexy black dress.

I clicked the television off at the set and crept over to Naomi. As I began tucking the blankets in, trying to make sure she was comfortable, her eyes opened.

"You're back! How was it?" She wiped her face.

She sat up and moved over, creating some space for me to sit down. I rubbed my face exhaustively and shrugged. "I'm not sure. I don't know what I'm feeling. This feels so complicated right now."

Naomi looked worried. "Do you want to talk about it? You've told me absolutely nothing about him."

I took in a deep breath and turned toward her. "Okay, I

want to tell you something but I want you to hear me out completely before you react."

I'd already decided I was going to tell her the truth. It was too heavy a secret now to keep it all to myself.

"The man I met for dinner tonight, was Silas Denton."

She gasped. Her eyes were wide in shock but I'd already made her promise not to say anything till she'd heard the whole story.

I continued, trying not to give up all together and run away. "As you know, we met at the fundraiser. I don't know how to describe it, I felt this instant connection with him. I've never felt this way about a man before, and so quickly. And then I found out who he really was and that made me sick to my stomach."

Naomi lowered her hand from her mouth. She was staring at me starkly. "But you still want him, despite knowing who he is?"

I gulped nervously, hanging my head low. I felt like I was deceiving myself, like I was deceiving everyone—most importantly the work I'd dedicated my life to. I looked up at her and nodded. "I do, I did...but I think it's over now. I got it out of my system. It was just one night and now I can move on."

"What do you mean you got it out of your system, Iris?" Naomi asked.

"I slept with him."

She was trying her best not to look disappointed but I could see it in her eyes. She threw her head back, looking up at the ceiling.

I reached for her arm. "Naomi..."

"Just please, Iris, will you please tell me everything?"

When she looked at me again, I saw that I'd hurt her

more because I'd kept all of it from her. We always told each other everything.

"Yeah, I'll tell you everything."

∼

The next morning, we woke up on the couch, leaning against each other, my neck stiff. I had no recollection of falling asleep but we apparently had dozed off at some point.

Bess was standing in front of us, staring at us with a gleeful smile on her face.

"Good morning!" she squealed and jumped on to the couch between us.

She wrapped herself in my arms and I kissed the top of her head.

"I'll make the coffee," Naomi said, after she'd exchanged kisses with Bess too.

"Chocolate chip pancakes?" I suggested.

Bess was excited, bouncing around the living room with a shrill laughter.

We all huddled in the kitchen together, making pancakes and coffee, and chatting. I'd told Naomi everything the previous night. Exactly what happened between Silas and me, the whole story he told me about his family, and then how I was the one who suggested that he take me home.

She was shocked at first, but then she agreed that I had done the right thing by accepting the check. It was a lot of money, and if it was genuinely coming from a good place, it would be a crime to deny that kind of help.

But Naomi was also in agreement with me that it was over between us.

Firstly, he was not the kind of man who would want anything more than a one-night stand, especially with someone who had a kid. Secondly, he had shown no interest in taking things any further.

Last and most important I didn't know if I could even see a future with him. It would be absurd. Other than the undeniable sexual chemistry between us, what else did we have in common? Yes, he was good with Bess, but that was on one occasion. He was trying his best to convince me to have dinner with him, and it worked.

When breakfast was ready, the three of us sat at the kitchen table and ate together. I was happy like that, it was comfortable. I had a decent job, I was doing the work that I loved, I had a beautiful and loving daughter, and a best friend I could trust. I'd decided a long time before that I didn't need a man to complete me, and that had not changed.

I laughed while Bess and Naomi talked about some cartoon character they both loved, mimicking it's voice. Sometimes Silas' face, his smell and his body flickered through my mind, but I did my best to brush those thoughts away. I knew it was only happening because he was still fresh in my mind. A few days...maybe even a few hours and I would forget about him. He'd be nothing more than one pleasurable mistake.

"Let's get you ready for school, Bessy, c'mon." I nudged her along after breakfast was done.

"I'll get the dishes and then head back home. Need to get out of these clothes before I go to work," Naomi said.

I smiled warmly at her. Bess had already run to her room so we had a moment to ourselves.

"Thanks for everything, Naomi. I don't thank you

enough for everything you do for me. And thank you for being so understanding and encouraging."

I gave her a hug and she hugged me back.

"Don't worry about it, hun, we all make mistakes," she said.

29

SILAS

Four days went by and I did everything I could to carry on with my life.

I rewrote the check the very next day in the office and sent it by hand to the agency. I wasn't expecting to hear back from Iris, and I didn't. She'd made it very clear to me that our evening together was a one time thing. That we got it out of our system and now we could move on.

It sounded right.

Logically, it made sense.

But if that were true, then why was I waking up every morning in my bed, covered in sweat after a night of fantasizing about her? I had no interest in going back to any of my usual joints. They were places I usually met women to bring home. I had a few other names on my phone who usually responded happily to my requests of booty calls, but they failed to interest me either.

It was only Iris on my mind and it felt like she was taking over my life.

At work I was thinking about her during meetings. I found myself drifting off during conference calls. Ever since

I'd shared our story with her, my disdain toward our father had increased.

I'd rescued him out of a rut. His business was over. His money was diminishing. Four years before, I got him to agree to a plan of setting up a legitimate business for the family, for Mom's sake.

Since then, I'd tried every day to clean our affairs out as much as possible.

I was the only one in the family who had truly forgiven him. But now I was beginning to doubt if he deserved my forgiveness at all. What would Iris have done if she was in my place? She wouldn't have forgiven him. She would have distanced herself from the family as much as she could.

I found myself wishing that she'd never figured out my name, that she had no clue who I was. If I just had a few more days with her before she knew, maybe we could have started something unstoppable.

I needed several drinks every night to make myself fall asleep, and I was going to work every day feeling like a shell of my previous self.

It was hard to describe exactly what I was feeling because I'd never felt it before, so I had nothing to compare it to.

Maybe Lena saw it in me too because she kept looking at me with sympathy.

On the fifth day, which was a crisp bright Fall Saturday morning, I woke up and decided I wasn't going to work that weekend. I was going to solve everything that was plaguing me. I was a problem solver, I always had been. It was what I was good at, what I was known for. The least I could do was take responsibility for my own problems and do something about them.

∽

I showed up at Iris' apartment and already knew it was a mistake as I walked up the steps. I knew I should have had respected her wishes and stayed away, but I couldn't help but wonder if she'd changed her mind. If she thought about me at all.

It was the middle of the morning, and since it was a Saturday, I hoped they were at home.

Iris opened the door just moments after I knocked. She was wearing a pair of jeans with rips in the knees and a tight turtle neck, her hair in a ponytail. She had a worn pair of Chuck Taylors on her feet, and was wearing no makeup. She was more beautiful like that than all dressed up.

She was smiling, obviously in the middle of saying something to her daughter. There was a cartoon show on in the background.

"Oh!" She exclaimed when she saw me standing at the door.

I had a hamper full of chocolates this time and I stretched it out toward her. I'd never felt like that before—excited and nervous at the same time.

"I'm not sure what I'm doing here," I said.

It felt even more awkward because I was in a suit while she was dressed so casually. Iris wiped her hands down the legs of her jeans and accepted the hamper from me.

"Hi, Silas. Bess will be happy to see you. We were just getting started on a cake. I've taken the day off from the cafe I work at," she replied in a casual tone.

"Is that Silas?" I heard Bess' voice in the background.

Just seconds later she was running up to me. I crouched down so she could come over and give me a hug, like we were long lost friends. I felt warm inside when she hugged me.

"How are you? It's been long. I brought chocolates," I said.

Bess was happy and bright and she caught me by my hand and led me into the apartment.

"We're baking a chocolate cake and Mommy says I can add whatever I want to the icing. I picked rainbow sprinkles and chocolate wafers because they're my favorite."

Bess was unstoppable. She was dragging me to the kitchen and I looked over my shoulder and saw Iris behind us, with her arms crossed over her breasts.

We hadn't had a chance to discuss me just showing up... again. I had no idea what she was thinking or what she wanted. Did she want me to leave?

Every time I caught her eye, she smiled politely and then looked away. The kitchen counter was covered with bowls of ingredients. There was flour everywhere. It didn't seem like either of them knew what they were doing.

"Have you made a cake before?" I asked Iris as I took my jacket off.

She shrugged and bit down on her lip.

"Okay, I'm taking the lead here. I used to bake with my mom all the time when I was a kid," I said.

30

IRIS

Silas and Bess did most of the baking. He seemed to be an expert at it, which was the last thing I was expecting from a Denton. They popped a perfectly looking chocolate cake into the oven and put it on a timer.

"When can we make the icing?" Bess asked while Silas dusted his hands.

"While the cake is cooling down. We can take a break for about thirty minutes," he said.

His jacket was off, his shirt sleeves were rolled up, his pants were covered in patches of flour, but he didn't seem to care. I wasn't sure whether to laugh at him or feel bad for him. It was just such an odd sight to see.

"Why don't you watch some TV, hun?" I suggested to Bess who was more than delighted about that.

When she went running out of the kitchen, I turned to face Silas. He was washing his hands in the sink.

"That felt therapeutic. Haven't baked a nice wholesome chocolate cake in years," he said. "Maybe the last one I baked was with my sister when she was about Bess' age."

"How old is she now?" I asked, smiling.

"Nearly twenty-three. She's much younger than me."

"So, she was very small when..." I trailed off, almost feeling bad for bringing it up.

"When Mom died? Yeah," he replied keeping his gaze turned from me.

I busied myself making coffee while he stood around in the kitchen. The past four days had been miserable. I thought I'd be over him by then. I thought it had meant nothing more than a one-night stand, but it was impossible to get him out of my mind. I couldn't stop thinking about him and everything he said.

I hoped to see him again, but never in a million years would I have imagined him in my kitchen, baking a cake with my daughter.

"Thank you for your donation. We are all extremely grateful at the agency. We'll be able to do some great work with it," I said, pouring coffee into two mugs.

"Thank you for accepting it."

He took the mug from me and we sipped our drinks slowly, barely glancing at each other.

"I'm sure you're wondering what I'm doing here." He finally addressed the elephant in the room.

"A little bit," I admitted.

He ran a hand through his hair. "I'm sorry I'm here, I just had to see you. I felt like it was unfair for us to just leave it like that."

I didn't know what I wanted to hear, but I didn't know what to expect either.

"Did you have more to say?" I asked but my voice came out as a whimper.

"Didn't you?" He asked, and I looked down at my coffee mug in embarrassment. Of course, I had more to say. I just didn't know if he wanted to hear any of it. In fact, I was *sure* they weren't things he wanted to hear.

I watched him silently as he took a few more sips of his coffee. "This is weird for me because I don't usually just show up at women's houses like this, after I've fucked them already."

That was a pretty bold statement and I looked up at him, feeling a bit surprised. "So why are you here?"

Silas put his mug down and stepped toward me. Immediately I had flashbacks of that night, pinned against the counter just like that. How desperately I'd wanted him that night. I looked up, holding my chin high, trying to hide my nerves. How would I explain it to Bess if she walked in?

He cleared his throat, keeping his eyes strong on mine. "Because I'm not sure what I want from you, Iris, and it's driving me crazy."

He was searching my eyes. His were dark and stormy again, dangerous.

"Silas, I have a daughter. I can't keep doing this with you," I whispered.

Our bodies were just inches apart. he was close enough to me to feel the warmth of his breath against my face. He clenched his jaw and took a step away from me.

"You're right, this is insane," he growled and ran a hand through his hair.

"I'm not free to make stupid decisions in my life. I had my chance to make them in my early twenties and I made loads of them. Now I have Bess and I have to think about her, even if it's nothing but a one-night stand. I have to think of the consequences."

Silas was holding my gaze firmly. He stuck his hands into the pockets of his pants. "I know and I wish this was as easy as me just walking away and never thinking about you again, but it isn't."

"What are you trying to say?" I asked.

I could feel my voice cracking. Over those previous four days, all I had thought about and fantasized about was what it would feel like if Silas was a permanent part of my life. What if he wanted me as more than...

He cut through my thoughts. "I don't know. I've never had this before. I've never taken anything with a woman this seriously, because there's always been some shit going on in my life."

"Are you saying that you want to..."

"I want to keep seeing you," he stated.

The timer on the oven went off. The kitchen was filled with the smell of chocolate cake and suddenly, it felt like I was in Paradise.

Bess came running into the room, excited to sample her cake and Silas and I stepped even farther away from each other.

"Gloves first!" He declared, switching on his cheerful voice for Bess.

It amazed me how much I didn't know about him, how much I'd underestimated him.

31

SILAS

We spent some time icing and decorating the chocolate cake, which was, of course, the best part for Bess. The cake turned out to be a great success and Iris cut out big generous slices and the three of us sat around the kitchen table eating it.

Iris and I still hadn't had a chance to really discuss our situation openly. I'd told her what I was feeling—that I was confused and unsure about everything, and she made it clear that we couldn't keep doing whatever we were doing because of Bess.

The last thing I wanted to do was put her in a tough situation, no matter how much I wanted to be with her.

After we were done eating our cake, it was past lunch time and Iris suggested that we all go out for lunch, something small from a food truck at the park.

"I have to go to the agency after that for a few hours and I'm taking Bess with me," she said, in a way that made it obvious that after the park she wanted me to leave them alone.

I definitely didn't want to overstay my welcome.

We left the apartment and walked together to the park. Bess was skipping and jumping in front of us, while Iris and I walked behind, maintaining a safe distance from each other.

"I'm afraid that Bess is already getting too attached to you," she said.

"I'm getting attached to her. She makes me feel like I've known her forever."

"Yeah, she has a way about her," Iris admitted with a smile.

"She's never really had a male presence in her life, no father figure. I can see that she's starting to look at you that way and I really don't want to hurt her."

I realized then that I knew nothing about her past. I didn't know who Bess' father was, what their relationship with him was like. I couldn't imagine her with another man either, it made me mad.

"I don't want to hurt Bess," I said.

We were walking into the park and Bess went straight for the swings. Iris had her hands in the pockets of her jeans. She looked casual and comfortable... and beautiful. A woman I would want to be seen with everywhere. The kind of woman I didn't even know I needed.

She was staring at her daughter silent for several moments before turning suddenly toward me. "So, what are we going to do, Silas Denton?"

I chuckled. "You don't have all the answers?"

She smiled and brushed some hair away from her face.

I stepped up closer to her. "I want to spend more time with you, get to know you, figure out what's going on between us. I have no idea what to do because I've never experienced this before, but I don't want to do it at the cost of that little girl."

She was looking into my eyes as I spoke.

"You think we could be more than just a one-night stand?" she asked.

"That is what I'm trying to say."

She started to smile and relief began to flood through me. Maybe she wanted the same things that I did.

"I haven't really done this in a while either," she said softly, stepping up closer to me.

Her face was just inches away. I could kiss her if I wanted to, but Bess could see us.

"So, we're just a pair of headless chickens running around clueless?" I asked.

She laughed. I was glad I could make her laugh. I couldn't help myself and reached over, tucking a piece of hair behind her ear.

She parted her lips like she wanted to be kissed.

"Before I do anything to you in front of Bess, which trust me, I definitely want to do right now, you should probably have a talk with her first."

Iris gulped and nodded.

"Yes, that's a good idea," she said and reached for my arm, just tugging my jacket with her fingers.

It was her way of showing me how much she wished we could be alone together. That's what I wanted too, but we had to make things more than just about sex. It was more than just about sex.

"I'm going to go now. You and Bess should have some alone time together like you originally planned, before I came over and crashed the party," I said.

"It's not like either of us are complaining."

"Will you have dinner with me again? Tomorrow night? I cook too, baking isn't my only skill in the kitchen." I laughed.

She looked impressed and nodded wildly. "I would love that. This time I'll tell Bess exactly where I'm going."

"I'll see you at eight?" I asked.

She chewed on her lip with a big smile on her face. I wanted to lift her up in the air and twirl her around. What was happening to me?

I walked over to Bess and gave her a quick hug and took my leave.

I didn't go near Iris again because I was sure I'd kiss her right there in front of everyone at the park. She waved at me as I walked out and I waved back.

Things were already starting to feel like a relationship. I was comfortable with her. She made me want to tell her everything, things I wouldn't have dreamed of telling another woman.

But Iris was different. There was something special about her, and finally, it was beginning to feel like I had a new purpose in my life. Like everything I was working toward would finally be worth it.

32

IRIS

I hadn't been in that good of a mood in a while, not even on the night of the fundraiser, and I was sure Bess could see it on my face.

We had a light lunch of sandwiches and milkshakes from the food truck near the park and then walked together to the agency. She seemed a little sad that Silas was gone and I told her she would see him again soon.

I was excited and looking forward to the next day.

What had happened that morning was definitely unexpected. He appeared at my door out of the blue with emotions I never thought he would have for me. I thought I was the only one with feelings, and those feelings were ones that only I shared. I had tried so hard to push them away.

Even though Silas had given me a personal version of his childhood and his family's history, the truth was, he was still a Denton. I wasn't positive that I could look past that despite the work I was trying to do. On the other hand, it all seemed so perfect. Like we were where the Universe wanted us to be.

I had watched him with Bess. His affection toward her

was honest and loving. Of course, I had initially questioned his intentions, which was only natural. I used to think of the entire family as monsters, pariah that had created the mess I was trying to clean up. But the longer I spent with Silas, the more I realized, he was human just like me. He had been through some extraordinary experiences in his life, and they had shaped and molded him into a strong, impenetrable man with a playboy exterior.

I could feel the connection we shared, and it was more than sexual.

I just needed to find a way to explain all of it to Bess, to make her see that Silas was going to be a more frequent part of our lives. I hoped she would understand what 'taking it slow' meant, and that she wouldn't grow too attached.

As much as I was attracted to him, as much as I was already building castles in the air—I wasn't naive enough to assume it would last forever. The truth was, I still knew very little about him. The only things I understood was what he told me. The rest was up to me to uncover.

As we walked up to the agency, I remembered that I would have someone else to talk to about everything. Naomi.

She wanted what was best for me, and she wanted me to move on with my life and someday settle down with a man who loved and cherished me. But I was pretty sure she would not view Silas Denton as that man, not until I helped her see things the way I was seeing them. Not until she saw how much he meant to me.

It brought a smile to my face when I thought about a cozy family dinner with Silas, Naomi, Bess and I. Those two would have a lot of differences to iron out, but I was hopeful. I was on cloud nine. I had a skip in my step.

Naomi was the first person I laid eyes on. She was

standing in the reception area with a clipboard in her hands, presumably waiting to greet any newcomers who were coming into the agency to talk.

But I stopped in my tracks when I saw her face. She looked like she'd seen a ghost, she almost looked afraid.

"Naomi? Honey? What's wrong?" I released my grip on Bess' hand and I rushed toward my best friend.

"I've been waiting for you. Where have you been? You're late!" She spoke robotically.

I searched her eyes, clamping my hands on her shoulders. "Yeah, sorry, I'm fifteen minutes late, we got carried away at the park. Are you alright? You look like you've seen a ghost…"

I allowed a soft nervous chuckle to escape my lips.

Naomi looked over my shoulder at Bess who was standing at a distance from us, watching us curiously.

"Naomi!" I said curtly this time.

She lowered her voice to a bare whisper. "He's here. I managed to calm him down and make him wait in one of the meeting rooms."

I was even more confused now. "He? Who is he? What are you talking about?"

For a moment I thought it was Silas but I couldn't imagine why he would leave the park and head straight over to the agency. And why did Naomi look so afraid? No matter how much she disliked Silas, she wasn't afraid of him!

She met my gaze now, widening her eyes even more. "It's *him*, Iris. He's back. We can't let him see Bess."

When I heard those words, I knew exactly who she was talking about and my heart turned ice cold. I gulped, trying to control the rising fear and anger inside me.

"Okay, you need to take Bess, take her back to the apartment and stay there," I whispered. "Go. Now!"

The last thing I wanted was for him to come out of the meeting room and see my daughter.

"Mommy?" Bess called out to me but Naomi went running over to her and scooped her into her arms.

"Hush, honey, we need to go, now. Mommy will come to us later," Naomi whispered to Bess.

I waved at her, trying to smile and seem casual but she'd seen the look of fear in my eyes already. I nodded at her but she didn't say anything back.

I waited till Naomi and Bess were both safely out of the building. I was sure she'd look after Bess and keep her safe. I hadn't seen him in four years. I'd started to forget what he even looked like, and now I was going to come face to face with him again.

I walked up to the meeting room. I could hear Sarah with a woman in the other room, having a session. I opened the door and saw him sitting on one of the plastic chairs, and I felt my heart leap out of my chest.

"Hello Ian."

SILAS

I left work early the next day because I'd never cooked dinner for anyone other than a family member before, and I wanted to be well prepared. The feeling was strange. I felt like a teenager trying to impress the girl he had crushed on for years. She made me feel like a kid again, like our love was the only thing that mattered.

I went to the grocery store and shopped for all the ingredients I thought I would need. I was going to give myself two hours to cook a delicious three course meal for two, one I was sure was going to impress her. She would never see it coming!

I couldn't believe things had worked out between us. I couldn't stop smiling.

Once at the apartment, I showered and changed into fresh clothes before I put the apron on and started cooking. On the menu was a roasted butternut squash salad, chicken breasts for the main course with goat cheese and a spinach stuffing, and some roasted Fall vegetables on the side. For dessert I was going to prepare a simple apple and blackberry crumble.

I'd grown up watching my mother cook fabulous meals for us everyday. She spent most of her time indoors because Dad preferred it that way. It was only later that we found out *why*.

While we had help around the house with everything else, cooking for the family was something Mom reserved for her. It was one of her favorite duties, and as the oldest son, I was always allowed to help.

Now, I had reason to cook again. I wanted Iris to see the other side of me, the parts that weren't visible to anyone else. What I kept hidden. For the first time in my life, I wanted someone else to see the real me.

I found myself humming while I cooked. Things were really turning around!

And just as I slipped the baking dish for the crumble in the oven, the intercom buzzed. It was too early for Iris, but the smile on my face proved I couldn't wait. It was Matty from the reception downstairs.

"Mr. Denton, your father is here to see you. He's taken the elevator upstairs but I just wanted to warn you," Matty said.

My father? In all the time that I'd been living here, he'd only visited me once. I wiped my hands down my apron, checked on the vegetables roasting, and untied it from the back, laying the apron over the chair. The doorbell rang and I rushed to open the door.

The faster he finished saying what he was there to say, the faster I could get him out of there.

"Hello son!" He greeted me and walked straight into my penthouse.

"Dad? What are you doing here?" I couldn't hide the surprise from my voice.

He stopped in the hallway and half-turned to look at me.

"Are you cooking?" he asked.

His eyes had grown wide in shock. I crossed my arms over my chest. "Yes, I am, as a matter of fact."

"For yourself or are you having some guests over?" he continued.

He'd never been this curious about my private life before. "How can I help you, Dad?" I asked him.

The last time we spoke was when I'd stormed out of his office in a temper, I wasn't sure I was ready to make peace with him yet. There were a lot of creases to be ironed out between us still, but that was not the time to do it.

My father sighed, turned, and walked toward my den. How did he even remember the layout of my place?

"I'm going to make myself a drink and then we can talk," he said.

I followed him there. "Talk about what? I'm kind of in a hurry here, Dad."

But that didn't stop him from walking over to my bar and start pouring himself a whiskey. "What is it son? You don't want to introduce me to your guest?"

I couldn't even imagine what Iris would say or do if she came face to face with my father. It would not be the ideal start to the night I had planned for her. The only reason we were having that date was because we'd managed to put the subject of my father on the back-burner for now.

"I need you to answer my question, Dad. Why are you here?" I had clenched my hands on my sides now.

I was usually pretty good at handling my temper with him, but lately, he was beginning to get on my nerves. "I came here because we need to talk, Silas. I feel like you're unhappy with me and we can't have that..."

He was sipping his whiskey and staring at me expectantly as he spoke. Like he wanted me to reassure him that I didn't have a problem with him. I hadn't realized that my father cared about what I thought of him.

"We can talk about it later Dad, at the office tomorrow maybe," I said, looking at my watch.

The last thing I wanted was for Iris to show up while he was still there. "No, I want you to just get it out. Tell me what you really fucking think of me, son! God knows your brothers have made it very clear to me already. They're too fucking high and mighty for our business."

Dad's face was turning red. He was angry. He gripped the glass tightly in his hand, like he was going to crush it right there.

"I told you what I think of you," I said and slipped a hand into the pocket of my jeans. "That you were a coward for sending me to the fundraiser instead of going yourself. And if you really want to donate to that charity, then you should have considered doing it anonymously. What made you think that an organization that works in the Southside hasn't heard of our family? Why would they accept the money from us?"

He drank some of his whiskey and nodded his head. "But I know they've taken the money."

"Yeah because I convinced them to!" I grunted.

Dad smiled, in a sly way, like he knew they would take the money all along. "That's the thing about the Southside, son, you don't know because you never really got to know it or the people who live there." He took a few steps towards me while I glared him down. "In the end, they're all the same. Just a bunch of greedy hungry scum of the Earth. What me and the others like me gave that neighborhood was the best they could have asked for."

I punched the glass out of his hands. It crashed on my marble floor and Dad stepped back startled.

"You helped spread addiction. You made it fucking impossible for even teenagers to avoid getting addicted. Your business was a disease!" I growled, moving toward him.

I watched as Dad clenched his jaw. He was glaring back at me. "You people will never understand."

"Get out of my house!" I pointed to the door.

I could hurt him right if he stayed there for a minute longer.

Dad pushed his hands into his pants and held his head up high. "Some day you'll thank me. All of you."

I followed him out of the den, down the corridor, and I banged the door shut after him.

I rushed back to the den to pick up the broken pieces of crystal off the floor. *Fuck*! What was going on with me? I'd never spoken to my father like that before. But he deserved to hear it. I knew that too.

Once I'd cleared the shards from the floor, I sat down next to the couch, on the rug, my arms supported by my bended knees. I wanted to see Iris. I couldn't wait to see her face in front of me. I wanted to tell her more. Reveal more of myself to her. There was still so much to say!

I didn't know what was going to happen with my dad, but I knew things were headed in the right direction with Iris and that was what was keeping me sane.

I checked on the food. I got everything ready. The dining table laid out in the dining room. The candles were lit, the wine was being chilled in the ice basket. I was ready to greet her at the door with a kiss, but Iris never showed up that night.

34

IRIS

When I walked into the meeting room that evening, Ian was sitting at my desk, on my chair, drinking water from my cup. He looked up at me and that initial look of anger and disgust turned to a sly smile.

Over the past four years, there wasn't much that had changed about Ian, except that his eyes looked brighter and his skin looked clearer. The last time I saw him, he was pretty much just skin and bones. It seemed like he'd been eating well lately.

"Well, well, look at you! All grown up, running your own business now," he said as he looked around the meeting room.

I left the door open behind me and didn't move any closer to him. "It's not a business, it's a charitable non-profit organization. I don't make any money from it."

If there was one thing I'd learned about Ian over the years, it was that he meant nothing as a real compliment. His hair was the same ginger color, his skin was pale as ever and it seemed like his freckles had multiplied. Had he been going to a gym too? He definitely looked more buff.

"Whatever it is, it has your name on the fucking front door, and yet that bitch Naomi acts like she owns the place!" He stood up from my chair, a grimace on his lips.

"What are you doing here, Ian?" I asked.

I tried not to let my voice crack. It wasn't like he could actually do anything to me, not inside my own office.

"You know why I'm here, Iris," he said.

I shook my head. "You'll have to tell me because I don't have a clue."

"You don't know why I'm here?" he asked as he took a few steps toward me. "The thought never crossed your mind that maybe you're keeping a father away from his daughter?"

I gulped and moved back towards the door. "You were never interested in her before, Ian, so no, the thought did not occur to me."

He came to a stop about a foot from me and nodded slowly. "You know what? You're absolutely right. I'm not going to deny it, but you see me now, right? You see that I'm clean. I've been clean for thirteen months, Iris. Things have changed."

My eyes flitted over his face. His eyes were clear, he was standing stock-still, he wasn't fidgeting, he looked like he'd been taking care of himself. Was he really telling the truth?

"So what?" I snapped defensively.

"So, I think it's time that Bess got to know her daddy," Ian said with that nefarious smile starting to spread across his face.

I felt like I was going to burst right there. How was I supposed to make a decision like that? After everything. After all this time.

Ian tipped his head to the side as he watched me. "I'm not going to force myself on you guys, Iris, but I want you to consider what would be best for our child. Tomorrow evening. I'm going to show up at your apartment. I'm hoping you'll let me in."

Then he left.

It was the first time Ian and I had spent any time together without screaming at each other. Maybe he was right, maybe things *had* changed.

~

I couldn't go to work the next day and I asked Naomi and Sarah to look after the agency for the evening. Bess could sense that something important was going to happen but I tried to keep the truth from her for as long as possible. I needed to prepare what I was going to tell her.

She was going to meet her father that evening. The last time she saw him, she was too little to remember anything about him. And since then, whatever questions she'd asked about her dad—I'd dodged them with vague replies. Even though I had tried to maintain a policy of openness and truthfulness with my daughter all her life, I'd never been able to tell her about her father and what really happened back then.

I didn't want to hurt her. I thought I was protecting her.

Naomi tried her very best to dissuade me from seeing Ian again. She fought with me all morning, trying to convince me with affection and logic. Naomi had always hated him, but I had made up my mind. I needed to stop lying to Bess. At some point, Ian was going to find a way to weasel his way back into her life. If it wasn't going to happen now because of me, he'd try it when she turned eighteen. When I could no longer keep them apart.

I preferred that the two of them get to know each other under my supervision. Naomi wasn't convinced, she wanted to stay with me at the apartment and give me moral support, but I sent her away.

I needed to do it alone. If I could handle Ian at his worst, I could handle him clean.

After lunch, I took Bess for a short walk and told her that we were going to have a special guest visit us. I told her she was going to meet her dad that evening. At first she seemed skeptical, but then excited. Why wouldn't she be? I couldn't blame her for wanting to get to know him. Seeing her reaction convinced me even more that I was doing the right thing.

Ian and Bess both deserved a chance. It didn't mean that my relationship with her was going to change in any way.

After our walk, we returned to the apartment and waited for him to show up. We didn't have to wait long.

A part of me was hoping faintly that he wouldn't. That maybe he'd change his mind or that maybe nothing had changed about him after all. But at exactly six, there was a knock on the door, and I saw him through the peephole.

Bess had changed into her prettiest dress was sitting on the couch, doing her homework. She looked up with a glowing smile as I opened the door.

Ian was dressed in a button down shirt tucked into dark jeans, his ginger hair was brushed back and styled, and he looked freshly shaven. I had no recollection of him ever looking like that. I was pleasantly surprised.

He was holding a box with a brand new Barbie doll inside.

"I wasn't sure what she would like," he said, with a big sloppy grin on his face.

"She would like that," I whispered and stepped aside.

Bess stood up from her couch.

"Hi Bess," Ian said as he walked into the apartment, holding the doll out toward her.

"Is that for me?" She asked.

She went over and took the box from him.

"What do you say, honey?" I asked.

"Thank you...Daddy," she murmured, a little hesitantly.

Ian looked at me, surprised. Maybe he hadn't expected me to tell her who he was.

"Come over here, let me see you" he said, crouching down to the floor.

Bess stepped up closer to him so he could pull her into his arms.

I watched from the door while they hugged. I could feel hot tears pricking my eyes. Why was I so emotional? Why did I want to cry? I'd spent so much time hating Ian and despising him, and now watching them hug was tugging at my heart strings?

Maybe it was because there was nothing I wanted more in that world than to make my daughter happy. As twisted as it was, Bess was happy right.

Ian was looking her over, amazed by her no doubt, the same way I was every day of my life. Bess was excited with her new doll and she'd already started talking in her usual friendly way. She knew how to put anybody at ease.

Then she stopped mid-sentence and looked up at Ian with a wide smile.

"Do you want chocolate cake? Me and Silas made it yesterday," she said.

"That sounds delicious! I would love some chocolate cake," Ian said, glancing at me with a smile.

That was when I remembered. Silas. I was supposed to have dinner with him. He'd be waiting for me at his apartment, he was going to cook for us! I hadn't even thought about him since I saw Ian in my office.

But what was I supposed to do?

I realized I didn't even have his phone number. No way of getting in contact with him and letting him know I wasn't going to make it.

But what was happening was far more important.

I couldn't screw this up between Bess and Ian, not for a guy.

~

I cooked a simple meal for dinner. Bess had already decided that Ian was going to have dinner with us. We ate sandwiches and milkshakes in the kitchen, then they talked some more. Bess showed him her collection of Barbies and other dolls.

From what I could see, the two of them had gotten along well, but then Bess was easy to get along with. Ian seemed a little distant at first, but that could have been because he wasn't accustomed to being around kids. He definitely wasn't a natural with her, the way Silas had been. He didn't exactly know how to talk to kids—but Bess didn't seem to mind.

She just seemed happy that she finally got to meet her dad.

It was a school night, though and she had to go to bed. Soon after dinner, I sent her to her room to brush her hair and teeth, and change into her pajamas.

Ian said he wanted to have a quick chat before he left so that would be a good time, while Bess was out of the picture.

He remained in the kitchen while I started to clear the plates and wash up.

"Thanks for opening the door first of all. I wasn't sure if you were going to make this easy for me or not," he said.

I had the faucet running and I put my rubber gloves on so I could start washing up. "I thought about it and decided I wasn't going to fight you on this because you have a right to meet your daughter. Besides, I knew how excited Bess would be to see you too. I just want what's best for her."

Ian was standing with his arms crossed, leaning against the kitchen door, watching me. I glanced at him. I thought I loved him once. I didn't see it anymore. What was it about him that attracted me to him back then?

Of course, I was young. I was twenty and had been living in the Southside all my life. Ian was not from around there, and he hadn't seemed like any of the guys from that neighborhood. Not like the guys I was used to dating. It didn't take me long to realize that I was wrong, he was exactly like them —except that he came from the other side of town and his family had money.

"You believe me, right? About how I've been clean for thirteen months now?" he asked, interrupting my thoughts.

I looked up at him, straight into his eyes and shrugged. "It doesn't matter to me, Ian. We're not together anymore. As long as you're not hurting or harming my daughter in any way, I don't really care."

"*Our* daughter, you mean?" His voice sizzled.

I heard an element of the old Ian, the guy I used to know from four years before—peep back into his voice again.

"Sure, yeah, our daughter."

"She is my daughter, Iris!" He growled and I met his eyes.

I nodded with clenched teeth. "Yes, she is, but you've barely been a father to her, Ian."

He was glaring at me like he couldn't believe what I was

saying. "And that's because you never let me! You've kept me away from her!"

I shut the faucet and turned to him, plonking one hand on my hip. "I kept you away from her because you were a crack addict, Ian. You were bad for her. You were bad for me!"

"I needed help," he growled moving toward me.

Flashes of memories from years ago came back. Ian and me alone in a kitchen, his eyes red, his speech distorted, his hand strong and rough around my neck. But I wasn't going to whimper away from him this time.

"You hit me. You hurt me. You nearly choked me to death!" I shouted and then clamped my mouth shut, realizing that Bess was in her room and she wasn't a baby anymore. She could hear. She could understand now.

Ian's nostrils were flared. "I was an addict. Things are different now."

"What do you want me to say? I let you have dinner with Bess tonight. What more do you want?"

Ian laughed. It was a sarcastic, cruel laugh. He wasn't really in a good mood. "You *let* me? You think you're doing me some kind of favor? I have as much rights over her as you fucking do!"

I shook my head and looked away. "I honestly thought tonight was going to be good for Bess, and it has been...and now..."

Before I saw it coming, Ian was gripping me by my shoulders. I gasped and stared at him with rounded eyes. A wave of fright had washed over me.

"I want to make this work with Bess. Don't you see that? I want to get to know my kid. I want her to trust me and love me," he said.

I looked into his eyes, and as much as I wished I could

hate him again, the way I did four years before—all I really saw was a miserable ex-addict. I saw the father of my child. A man who was now begging me to give him a second chance.

He released his grip on my arms and stepped away. "Sorry. Sorry about that. I should go. I'm going to go."

He was fumbling with his words.

I followed him out of the kitchen as he rushed toward the front door.

"Tell Bess I had to go if she's still awake. Thank you, Iris, really, thank you for this. I mean it. We should talk again. I hope you'll talk to me again."

He sounded flustered and weak and within moments, he was out of the door and running down the stairs. I waited a few moments before I shut the door and breathed a huge sigh of relief.

That was a small speed bump in the kitchen. It was unpleasant, but nothing like it used to be. I still wouldn't be comfortable to leave him alone with Bess, I didn't completely trust him—but the answer to the question of whether Ian had changed and made a recovery, was yes.

I couldn't be the person who denied an ex-addict a second chance.

That was what my life's work was all about.

35

SILAS

The next day I stormed into the cafe where Iris worked. This was the first time I'd taken an actual lunch break from work in years.

I saw Iris right away. She was the manager and standing behind the counter making notes in a small notepad. She was dressed in a white shirt and dark pants, her hair was tied tightly in a neat braid and she looked more professional than I'd ever seen her.

She looked up at me when I walked in. The café was busy and noisy and she quickly walked around the cafe and headed toward me.

"What the Hell happened to you last night?" I asked before she'd even come to a stop in front of me.

"I'm so sorry about last night, something came up, last minute and I didn't have your phone number." she said.

She looked sincere.

"Can we talk outside? This place is too noisy," I said.

Iris looked over her shoulder like she was checking on a few things and nodded. We headed out of the cafe.

I was relieved to see her, glad she was fine. "When you

didn't show up last night, I didn't know what to think. My best guess was that you'd changed your mind."

We walked over to a small table under an umbrella outside the cafe and sat down. When I said that, she looked away and I knew things weren't as smooth as I'd hoped either.

She shook her head and then chewed on her lip. "I haven't, that's not what it is. I've just...last evening I had some things to take care of. It involved Bess. I couldn't come and see you and if I had your phone number, I would have let you know."

She met my eyes this time and I could see she was nervous. Something was going on. "What happened?"

She gulped and shook her head. "Nothing you need to bother yourself with."

My brow furled. "Something at the agency?"

"No," she said meekly.

"Okay. You don't have to tell me. I just needed to know you were okay," I said.

Iris clasped her hands together on her lap and nodded her head. "I'm okay, it wasn't like that. I just...have a lot of things to deal with right now and not enough hours in the day."

I watched as she rubbed a hand over her face in frustration.

I wanted to help. For the first time in my life, I was actually in the company of a woman who wasn't my sister, who I wanted to help. I could have sat there listening to her talk for hours but it didn't seem to be what Iris was interested in doing.

"Okay." I sat back in my chair.

Iris had essentially closed herself off to me. I wasn't sure what more I could say to her. Something was going on in her life that she was unwilling to share with me. Could I really blame her for that? It wasn't like we were really in a relationship. We were just starting something off, beginning an exploration.

She was sitting uncomfortably, at the edge of her seat with her head hanging low. "I really don't know what to say to you right now, Silas."

"Is there anything I can do to help you?" I asked.

She shook her head without looking at me. "No, I really need to figure this out on my own."

"And you can't tell me anything? And I can't help you with anything?" I knew my tone was irritable.

I felt like suddenly my hands were tied.

She looked up at me but said nothing. I stood up from my chair. "I'm guessing you don't know when we'll be seeing each other again either."

She didn't stand up but she looked up in my direction. "I just don't...I can't think straight right now, Silas. I don't have the headspace to..."

I nodded. "Sure, yeah, I understand. You have shit to deal with."

"I'm sorry I can't be any clearer with you. I wish I could tell you more but I need to sort this out first."

"It wasn't going to work, was it?" I asked.

She gulped, looking sheepishly at me. "I can't predict the future."

I shook my head, shoving my hands in my pockets. "I wish we were just honest with each other from the beginning. You were never going to get past my dad or my family name. You were giving me a chance because...why? I wrote you a check? The sex was good?"

Iris jumped up from her chair. Her nostrils were flaring with anger now. "Is that what you really think?"

I was already starting to walk away. "I don't know what to think, Iris. Right now, what I know is that this isn't going to work and we were stupid to even think we could try."

She stared after me, shaking her head gently like she couldn't believe me.

In my head, the only thought repeating itself was that this could be the last time I would ever see her. I stared back at her for as long as I could and then I flipped around and stormed away.

I wasn't even headed in the direction of my parked car. I just wanted to get away from her. I didn't want her to see the disappointment in my eyes.

What was I thinking?

Why did I even assume, even for a moment, that I could make a relationship work?

Hadn't I learned my lesson from my dad?

36

IRIS

Naomi walked with me back from the agency to the daycare center where I was supposed to pick up Bess.

"And now what? Is he a part of your lives?" she asked after I explained everything to her.

I shrugged. "I don't know yet, Naomi. I'm just trying to take this one day at a time. He appeared back in our lives out of nowhere!"

As expected, she was not happy with the fact that I had let Ian spend any time with Bess. "And you forgot about your date with Silas! And you turned him away today!"

I gave her a look. "You don't even like him."

"He is definitely a better idea than Ian. Historically speaking, we know that already," she argued.

I hung my head as we walked along in silence. "I really don't know how to deal with this, I'm so confused. I mean, isn't this what we tell the people who come to us at the agency? That everyone deserves a second chance? Addicts alike. That you could have a life, a second lease after your addiction."

She was listening to me silently and spoke sometime after. "Yeah, but Ian is different. He was never interested in Bess. He wanted you to have an abortion. He was hateful and cruel toward you."

I knew she purposely didn't mention the night when he tried to choke me. She didn't want to bring those hurtful memories back, but I knew what she was talking about and I knew she was right. "But that was four years ago, when he was still using. Living here on the Southside, did that to him. He moved here because of me..."

Naomi stopped and grabbed my arm. "Don't you dare do that to yourself, Iris! What Ian became was never your fault. You never *made* him get involved with that crew. You never made him take drugs. That is all on him."

We were standing out front of the daycare. "He says he's been clean for thirteen months, Naomi."

"And what about Silas?" She asked me. "I hadn't seen you that excited in a long time. I don't know what it is but he knows how to make you spark up, light on fire."

I looked down at my feet embarrassedly. "I can't focus on anything else right now. I can't think about him. Besides, Bess needs me. What was I thinking? I can't get into a relationship right now. I don't have time for it..."

Naomi was looking at me like she pitied me. She opened her mouth to speak but I interrupted her.

"I should go in and get Bessy," I said and I quickly waved goodbye to her and walked away.

I knew she meant well, but right then, I just needed to think about everything with a clear head. I needed to be alone.

∼

*B*ess had a lot to say as we were walking back home. She said she'd told a lot of her friends in class that she'd met her daddy the previous evening.

We were walking holding hands and I could feel the happy energy coursing through her veins.

I wanted to ask her what she thought of Ian, I'd been trying all day to think of what words to use—but I figured that I didn't need to actually ask her. She was making it very obvious how she felt about him.

"Are you happy to see him?" I asked her eventually, just to confirm.

If Bess was happy to have him as a part of her life, it didn't matter what Naomi or anyone else thought of my decision. I was always going to do what was best for my daughter. She nodded her head wildly, excited and happy that we were discussing her father openly.

I hadn't asked her the same questions about Silas, I didn't think I needed to because we were going to take our relationship slow. Besides, I didn't need to ask Bess what she thought of him because she'd made it pretty obvious that she liked him, too.

Silas, who was a complete stranger to us and had no connection to our past—had been able to spark us up. That wasn't something that happened often.

But now it was over.

I couldn't think about him without recalling that look he gave me at the cafe as he was walking away. Like he'd known all along that things were never going to work. Like we were just kidding ourselves by even trying.

Yes, we had hurdles and problems, and there was the matter of his family—but the only reason I even wanted to make it work with him was because of how attracted I was to him. Because of how he made me feel, and how happy he made Bess.

But it seemed like he'd pegged us for disaster a long time before. He'd assumed from the start that we were never going to work. He was right. Why were we even trying then?

Bess and I walked the rest of the way home and settled into the apartment for the evening. After dinner, we ate some of the leftover chocolate cake. It made me think of Silas again and of the afternoon he'd spent with us there. I thought about how I blushed every time I looked at him.

I could still remember that fluttering feeling in my chest when I first saw him walking toward me at the fundraiser. How I felt like the luckiest woman in the world because he had chosen to notice me. No other man had made me feel like that before, like I was the only woman in the world.

Sitting there in the kitchen, staring at the cake, I didn't feel so lucky anymore. My shoulders felt heavy with the weight of the decisions I was going to have to make.

It wasn't just about Silas and me anymore, it was about the future of my daughter's life. It was just bad timing.

37

SILAS

I was a mess. Was that what a bad breakup was supposed to feel like? Except for the fact that it wasn't really a breakup. We weren't in a relationship in the first place.

She said she was dealing with personal shit, which she didn't want to disclose to me. She also said she didn't know when we could see each other again, and yet, when I told her I knew all along it wasn't going to work—she looked hurt and upset. Like she didn't want me to walk away.

So, what did she want me to do?

Beg?

Keep calling her?

Follow her around everywhere until one day she had time for me?

I wasn't an expert at relationships, sure, but even I knew when my chain was being yanked around. I should have known better than that. I should have known I wasn't just magically going to stumble across the woman of my dreams.

I locked myself in my office the next day, burying myself in work.

I was both angry and upset. I needed to distract myself with paperwork and research, and I made sure Lena canceled all my meetings. There was no way I could meet people.

It was around midday, when I'd finally managed to calm myself. Lena knocked on my door and said there was someone there to see me. I growled at her, reminding her how I'd asked for my schedule to be wiped clean for the whole day.

"It's your sister, Mr. Denton," she said assertively, because somehow, she knew I wouldn't say no to that.

"Sadie?" I said her name, as if I hadn't heard it out loud in decades.

She obviously had just come from the airport. There was a line of suitcases behind her. As soon as she saw my face, she came charging at me. I had barely been able to stand before she flung herself at me.

"Silas! Oh my God! You couldn't look any grumpier if you tried!" She clung from my neck for a moment and I patted her back.

"You're alive," I exclaimed.

I was genuinely delighted to see her. There wasn't a single other soul in the world that could have made me feel better in an instant.

Sadie smiled, propping herself up on the edge of my desk. "No big brother, I didn't get poisoned by Cobras in India, or run over by elephants in Sri Lanka. Let's not perpetuate any stereotypes here."

"You look great!" I said.

She was glowing, she was tanned to perfection, she looked healthy and as carefree as always.

"Can't say the same about you," she replied, arching her brow.

She may have been more than a decade younger than me, but nobody knew me like my sister did.

~

I took her out for a coffee at a hipster cafe near the office.

"Thought this place would suit you," I said when the waitress brought us our coffees in mason jars.

Sadie rolled her eyes. "Just because I went traveling around South America and Asia alone doesn't turn me into a avocado toast eating hipster!"

I tasted some of the coffee and it was nice. At least they knew how to roast and grind their beans. Sadie sat back in her chair and drew in a deep breath. "So, what is going on with you, big brother? You look like a man who has lost at love."

Was it really that obvious? Could she smell it off me? Her statement made me shift in my seat uncomfortably. "There's just been some things going on at the office, you don't want to hear about it. Things with Dad and money and the business."

I was quickly using words I knew she was allergic to. But she kept staring at me like she knew I was lying.

"So your current situation," she continued, drawing circles with her hand in front of my face. "It has nothing to do with a lady friend?"

"Lady friend? What does that even mean?" I chuckled.

"Why do I get the feeling that you've finally found a woman to date." She was poking at me in that cute little sister way she always did.

"Who are you getting this information from, Sades?" I asked.

She shrugged. "Nobody. It's just a feeling I have. I guess I'm wrong."

"You *are* wrong!" I stated, a little more aggressively now, which I knew was going to pique her curiosity even more.

"You have surprisingly, always been calm about work and Dad and the business. None of us know how you do it, which is why this worries me," she said, in a softer voice now.

I could sense her trying to search my eyes. Her scrutiny was making me deeply uncomfortable. "I'm getting older. Shit bothers me more these days. What can I say?"

Sadie nodded and shrugged it off. It wasn't that she'd bought my explanation, it was just that she was going to let it go until she decided it was time to talk about it again. Unlike our brothers, Alex and Miles, who like me, had no interest in talking.

I watched my sister knock her coffee back and then rub her mouth with the back of her hand like she'd just drank some juice.

"Let's go. Let's do this," she said, banging her fist on the table and standing up.

"Do what?"

"Let's go say hi to Dad. I'm sure he'll hear I'm back and he'll expect me to drop by," she said.

I hadn't seen dad in days, not since he came to the apartment that night. Maybe it was good. Sadie would be the perfect buffer between us to diffuse the tension.

38

IRIS

I didn't know where Ian got my phone number from, but he called me to set up a day and time to meet Bess again. He said he wanted to meet her soon because he wanted to spend as much time with her as he could. The next day being a Saturday, I agreed to fix up a plan for them.

We would go to the park together, where I could sit on a bench and read a book and watch them playing together at the same time. That way they could get some time alone.

I truly was trying to do my best to make it as smooth and easy for both of them as possible. If Ian really had changed as a person, if he was clean—our daughter didn't need to know about his past yet and he deserved a second chance. Who was I to come between them?

When I told Bess, she was excited for the next day. For me, it was nothing but nerves.

The next day Bess was teaming with excitement. We were going to meet directly at the park and she wanted to go as early as possible and wait for him there. As we were walking in, I stopped and knelt down in front of her.

"Baby, I want you to have a really good time today, but there is something that I also want you to remember," I said.

I was trying my best to not sound overly serious and scare her.

Bess tilted her head to one side and looked at me curiously.

"What is it Mommy?" she asked and reached over gently touching my face.

I clutched her hands and held them tightly. "I want you to spend time with your daddy, and I'm very happy for you honey, but I want you to remember that this could change soon. Before you get too attached. Just take your time to get to know him. Do you understand what I'm saying?"

I tucked some of her dark locks behind her ear while she stared at me, even more confused now. How was I supposed to teach maintaining distance to a six year old? Especially one who loved to get to know people.

"Okay Mommy," she said, even though I wasn't sure if she really did understand or not.

I smiled at her. "Okay honey, but most of all, just have fun, okay?"

She nodded her head and we walked into the park. Ian was true to his word and waiting for us there by the swings.

He threw his arms open for her and Bess ran into them. He had gotten her another new toy, a unicorn.

Ian and I spoke briefly. He wasn't willingly making eye contact with me, which I figured was because of our last conversation. Maybe I shouldn't have been that hard on him. Maybe it was a part of his recovery and he was really trying.

I told them I would leave them alone and I walked over to the closest bench and took out a book to read.

Bess seemed perfectly happy to be spending time with her dad, and I was perfectly happy for her.

∼

After they'd been playing together for over an hour, Ian left her to keep playing with a few of her friends and came up and sat down beside me on the bench.

I put my book down on my thigh and he looked at me with a smile. "She's so great. I can't believe I missed all this!"

He actually looked happy and proud, just the way Bess made me feel all the time. "Yeah, she's a miracle child. I don't know what I've done to deserve a kid like her."

Ian nodded and looked away from me. "I want to be there for her from now on."

I gave an uneasy smile, looking out at her. "Good, great, I'm sure she'll like that."

He turned to look at me. "I mean it, Iris. I'm clean, I'm back living with my folks again, I'm going to start working at the family business soon. I can do this. I can really be there for her this time."

I nodded, secretly admiring the determined look in his eyes. "I'm happy for you, that you finally got your shit together, Ian."

He ran a hand through his wavy ginger hair and stuck his hands into the pockets of his zipped up sweatshirt. "It's weird to be back here, in this neighborhood. Brings back memories when things weren't so good for me."

I knew what he was talking about but I decided to remain quiet. "I had to get out of here, you understand? To save myself?"

He looked at me again and I nodded.

"I would have been there for her if I could, but I couldn't. I had to save myself first. Take care of myself."

I nodded again. "You did the right thing. Bess is happier to have you in her life now."

I was trying to be supportive of him, the way I would have been toward anybody from that neighborhood who came to the agency for our help. I didn't remind him of those instances when he'd pushed it too far. Of how I'd thrown him out of our home and told him to stay away from our daughter.

Ian stood up from the bench again. "I better get back to her."

I watched him running back to Bess who was grinning from ear to ear.

I remained sitting on the bench for the rest of our time at the park, watching them play. I still wasn't completely sure about Ian and his recovery, but I was glad he was trying and I was glad I was giving him another chance.

At least for our daughter's sake.

But that didn't mean I wasn't thinking about Silas too, and wishing he was there with me. I just couldn't complicate Bess' life any further than it already was.

39

SILAS

It was good having Sadie back in town. She helped me stay distracted and put me in a better mood, reminding me that at least I had one person who I could still talk to.

She continued to look at me funny now and again, and I could sense she was trying to figure out if anything was going on in my life involving a woman. But we didn't speak about it anymore. I made it clear to her that I had nothing to talk about.

Our short meeting with Dad the other day, when Sadie had dragged me to his office, had been cold and curt. He was open and friendly toward her, but closed off toward me. Once again, Sadie could sense something was going on between us.

Three days went by. Sadie was living in my apartment until she figured out what she was going to do next. I still had to go to work to make sure the upcoming project was on track and running smoothly. The project could change everything for our company.

With this new development, our business would be officially and completely clean. We'd have no connections and no monetary ties to the old drug business in the Southside. It would be over for good.

I wished I could tell Iris, I wanted her to know, but there was no way. It was over between us, she made that very clear.

So, when I saw her standing outside my office building at nine in the morning on a chilly Wednesday, I thought I was hallucinating.

I saw her as soon as I pulled up out front of the building. Sid, the valet, quickly came over to take my keys from me so he could go park my car in the garage.

Iris looked up from her phone and our eyes met. She was bundled up in a thick wooly coat and a chunky purple scarf. Her long dark hair was left loose, her green eyes looking big and bright. Seeing her first thing in the morning was like a breath of fresh air. She had no idea the effect she still had on me.

It was bordering on cruel.

We met on the sidewalk, stepping out of the way of the foot traffic going up and down the street. She had a paper cup of coffee in her hand.

"Hi," she said.

Her cheeks were flushed pink from the chill.

I was concerned. "What are you doing here? Did something happen? Bess okay?"

She grinned and nodded. "Everything's okay. I was on my way to the café for my shift, but then I decided to come here and talk to you instead. Was that a mistake?"

I was standing close to her, over her, and she had to crane her neck to look up at me with her big delicious eyes. I could devour her. My cock moved in my pants. I hadn't been with, or even thought of, another woman since I first saw Iris.

"Do you want to come up to my office?" I asked her.

She shook her head. "This won't take long. I have to hurry to work anyway."

I wanted to reach for her face, stroke her cheek. Even though we both knew that a relationship would never work, it didn't mean the spark was gone. It didn't mean that I stopped wanting her in my bed.

"Okay, let's go for a walk then," I said.

I gave one quick sweeping look up my office building as she took my arm. I was going to be late for the conference call that was scheduled for nine-fifteen, but I discreetly reached into the pocket of my coat and turned off my cell phone so Lena couldn't reach me.

Iris and I walked slowly together on the pavement. It was a busy Chicago morning. Everyone was in a rush to go to work, to get somewhere...and the two of us were just walking together, trying to slow down time.

"I wanted to clarify something with you, Silas. Regarding what you said the other day to me when you were leaving. I didn't agree to go on a date with you because I felt grateful for the check, and neither did I think we were doomed from the start." She kept her head down as she spoke and I clenched my jaw while I walked beside her.

"Then what were we doing?"

She looked at me and quickly looked away. "Giving us a shot? I thought we were genuinely going to try. I felt a connection with you...I feel..."

"But then something happened?"

"Yes," she admitted.

We were squeezing together through the crowds, finding it difficult to stay together. I grabbed her by her arm and pulled her away from the crowd and toward a building's front.

She pasted herself to the wall and I pushed myself into her. There were layers of warm clothing between us. Iris breathed hard and mist formed from her mouth as she stared up at me.

I clutched her face by both cheeks and leaned into her. Our lips met. I stroked her mouth with mine, my tongue slipping in and tasting her delicious sweet taste again. She melted into me and it didn't matter that there were all those people around us, pushing into us, tripping on my feet. All I could do was stand with her like that and go on kissing her.

We were both breathless when I pulled away from her. Iris' eyes glistened. She licked her lips like she wanted to taste me again.

"What is going on with you?" I asked, tenderly stroking her cheeks.

The tip of her nose was pinkish red now, like she was forcing back her tears. She looked up at me again with a strain in her eyes. "There's so much about me you don't know, Silas."

40

IRIS

I couldn't resist kissing him back. With his swept back dark hair and those glittering blue eyes, he was more irresistible than ever. He was dripping masculinity. He was tall, strong, and powerful. I felt safe when I was with him, warm and cared for... even though things were going so massively belly-up for us.

Was that why I went there? Because I felt a deep physical need for him? Because I wanted to know if he still wanted me in the same way? So, what if he did? That didn't really change anything between us.

"Why don't you tell me?" he asked, breaking through my thoughts.

"I wouldn't even know where to begin," I said.

Some rowdy passerby pushed into him and he moved closer to me. Our bodies were now pinned together. My cup of coffee had fallen out of my hand a long time before. There was no space between us with my back pressed to the wall. There was no escape.

His voice was patient. "Why don't you begin by telling

me what happened that night? When I was waiting for you with a three-course meal."

I licked my lips nervously and tried to avoid his eyes. "My ex, Bess' dad...his name is Ian. He showed up out of the blue and demanded to spend time with her."

I had no clue how I even managed to get those words out. I hadn't planned on telling him, but now he knew. I saw how his brows crossed.

"I'm sorry...I should have..." I fumbled.

He shook his head. "I'm not an idiot, Iris. It's not like I assumed Bess came out of nowhere. I was fully aware that you have an ex, I guessed he was out of your life."

"He was! He has been for four years. He just turned up at the agency...and he claimed that he's been clean." I searched his eyes as I said those words.

There was a moment of recognition on his face. "*Clean?* You mean he was an addict?"

I nodded and looked down at my feet. Silas released his grip on me and ran a hand through his hair. "Shit!"

I pressed my eyes close. It was hard to talk about.

He was still slightly oblivious to the magnitude of his family's outreach. "I didn't know, you should have told me, how our business affected your life personally."

I opened my eyes and glared at him. "It affected everyone's life on the Southside, Silas. There aren't many people in that neighborhood whose lives *haven't* been affected by it in some way, even if they're not addicts themselves."

He breathed in deeply and nodded.

"What happened with him in the past?" Silas asked, peering into my eyes now.

It was a long story, so much had happened in that phase of my life. How was I going to tell him all that in gist? "I met him when I was twenty. I grew up there, he didn't. He made some friends on the Southside and started hanging around my neighborhood."

Silas was trying to carefully follow the story. "Where did he grow up?"

"Somewhere around here, his folks are rich, legitimate businesspeople. I never really met his family because they kicked him out once they found out he was an addict. We got into a relationship pretty fast. I thought he was cool and smart, and that maybe someday he'd be able to take me out of that place."

I tried to hold back the tears that were pooling in my eyes. It was embarrassing and sad to recall how foolish and naive I'd been back then. I actually thought Ian was going to save me!

Silas was watching me intently. He didn't say anything more but I could see it in his eyes—he was urging me to go on. It was strange but comforting somehow to be discussing something that personal out in the open like that, with swarms of people around us. Nobody was interested in eavesdropping. They all had somewhere important to be.

I continued with a shaking voice. "At first I didn't realize he was using. I thought he was different from everyone else because of his education and where he came from. He got a job at the same diner that I worked at. We were having fun together, playing house. We rented a small apartment above a garage."

I couldn't look Silas in the eye anymore, but he was staring at me, I could feel it. Did he pity me? Did he think I was an idiot? I knew I should stop, I was digging myself a deep hole.

But once I started talking, spilling my guts, I couldn't stop. "Then I found out he was using, his behavior had changed. He was skipping work, skipping our dinners together. I found the needles and the syringes in the bathroom. I freaked out. I'd dealt with it all my life, watched my only brother cave in. I couldn't be with a guy who was doing the same thing...but then I found out I was pregnant, just when I thought I was going to kick him out."

Silas sighed. He squared his shoulders and looked away from me. It was like he was frustrated too. Frustrated for me.

"So, you didn't leave him then?" he asked.

I hung my head, ashamed. I knew, in retrospect, that was a bad decision. "I didn't think I could do it alone. I thought I'd die if I had to do it alone. I told him about the baby and he seemed happy at first. He promised he'd get clean."

Silas rubbed a hand over his face and shook his head. "What did he do to you, Iris? Did he hurt you? Did he hurt Bess?"

His voice was deep and threatening now and his eyes were dark and narrowed.

I breathed deeply. "He was aggressive and angry. He never got clean. He stole money from me. Never spent any time with Bess..."

"Did he hurt you?" He interrupted me again.

I gulped and stared into his heavy dangerous eyes. "Once. He pushed me against the wall and tried to choke me. He was high. He had no idea what he was doing."

"Fuck!" Silas growled, stepping to the side and punching the brick wall with his bare knuckles.

It shocked me and I flinched, bringing my hands up.

"Silas!" I squealed seeing the blood on his knuckles. "I kicked him out after that! I made sure he was never coming near Bess again!"

41

SILAS

I felt like I was losing my mind. Just hearing about the shit that Iris had gone through, what her ex had put her through...the fact that he'd actually hurt her!

I could feel rage coursing through my veins. I wanted to find him, make sure he knew he could never come close to Iris and Bess again.

"So, what is he doing back here now?" I growled.

Iris licked her lips nervously. "It's been four years. He held up his end of the bargain. I told him to stay away from us and he did. He never tried to contact me, never tried to see Bess."

"But now. What about now?!" I growled again, raising my voice over the sound of all the traffic.

Her voice was panicked. "He's only back now because he's clean. He's back living with his parents. He says he's going to start working at the family business too. He's really pulled his life together."

"And you think he deserves to be a part of your lives now?" I knew I sounded threatening.

I was standing too close to her. My body was nearly covering hers. My hot breath was falling on her face.

I knew I could be intimidating in that position, but Iris kept her chin up and she looked me straight in the eye. "He wants to be a part of our daughter's life. Bess had been living with the absence of a father for the past four years. She didn't remember him and now she's so happy to see him again. He's actually making an effort."

"Are you fucking serious, Iris?" I couldn't believe it.

There I was, trying to push back a burning desire to kill the bastard and she was letting him back into their lives. In their home!

"What else am I supposed to do?" she squealed.

I thrust my arm out, pointing down the street. "Throw him out! Tell him he can't see her. Call the cops!"

"Call the cops for what? He's done nothing. He's clean. He doesn't even smoke around her. He buys her presents. He plays with her and laughs with her. He's trying his best to be a good dad." She was putting her gloves back on.

I fisted my hands in my pockets and shook my head. "He hurt you, Iris. He actually tried to choke you."

"He was high. You have no idea what being an addict can do to your brain," she snapped.

I looked at her angrily. "Are you seriously defending him right now? You want to feel sorry for him? For putting your life and your newborn baby's life in danger?"

Iris' eyes filled with tears and I knew I'd said the wrong thing, in the wrong way, but that was exactly what I wanted to say. I just wanted her to see how fucked up all this was.

"I want to give him another chance!" she cried.

"Another chance at what?" I shouted back.

"Fatherhood!"

There was a silence between us. Maybe she was right...

maybe he did deserve another chance at fatherhood. All I could think about was him, this faceless man, with Iris and Bess. I couldn't do it. I couldn't keep imagining that. It was going to drive me nuts.

"So, you want to be a family again?" I asked, in a softer voice now.

Iris scoffed. "That is not what I'm saying. That is definitely not what I'm saying! I think Bess deserves to get to know her father, and if he has put in this much of an effort to clean himself up—then he deserves a chance with her too. Not with me. I don't have any feelings for him. I don't even remember what I saw in him."

I took a few steps away from her. I was feeling too warm now, like I was burning up under all these clothes.

"But you and me are off the table too," I stated.

Iris' nose turned red again. "This is a really complicated time for Bess. She's taking it like a trooper, but I don't want her feeling torn between you and Ian. Not right now before she's even established a relationship with her father. And if you and I are going to have any kind of a relationship, I can't keep my daughter out of it either."

I nodded and looked away from her. "Why did you come here today, Iris? Telling me all this."

I knew it was a legitimate question. We weren't exactly friends. She didn't see a future for us together. So, why was she here? Iris looked like she was about to cry but I held myself back. This thing with me was not what she wanted. "Because I thought you deserved an explanation for why I couldn't make it to dinner that night, and why I abruptly backed away from you."

I stepped away, staring off in the distance. "Okay, and you've given me your explanation."

"Yes, I have..." she said softly.

"So, I'm going to walk back to my office now and you should get to work," I said.

We'd kissed once already today, so I needed to keep my distance.

"I guess so," she whispered.

I barely heard her over all the noise around us. I just saw her plump perfect lips move.

I looked her over and took one last good look at her. "Take care of yourself Iris, and take care of Bess like I know you will."

"You too, Silas," she replied in that same soft voice.

I turned from her and started to walk away.

My phone was still turned off in my pocket and I had no intention of turning it back on any time soon. I walked past my office building and I kept going.

42

IRIS

I shouldn't have gone to see Silas.

I was late for work. I was all worked up. I was turned on and angry at the same time, and I realized it was only him who could make me feel all those things at once.

I'd spent several days just trying to get over him. Trying to get past that nagging feeling in the pit of my stomach that I needed to see him again. That somehow, if I met him and told him everything—he would make everything better.

But, how could he?

We weren't in a relationship. He had no authority or power over me, and I didn't have any over him. And now he had made it very clear to me what he thought—he was in the same camp as Naomi. He did not support my decision to let Ian back into our lives.

I was on the L, back to the café so I could get started on my shift. I was standing even though there were a few empty seats around. I was trying to steady my racing heart but it was beating out of control.

Suddenly, it felt like it was six years before...when I had nobody to help me, nobody's support. When it was just me and Bess against the world. When I was the only one giving Ian a chance, because he was the father of my child, because it was the drugs to blame and not him.

Naomi and I were friends even back then, we were close and she never got along with Ian. Every time she happened to come across him, she reminded me how I could have any other man if I wanted to. I reassured her Ian was good for me, good for the baby, and that he was trying his best to pick himself off the ground. I didn't give her the full picture because I didn't want her to feel sorry for me. I didn't want her to see me as a pathetic weak creature.

But that night when Ian was so high that he didn't know he was choking me, when he could have killed me, I finally called her and told her everything.

Ian had stumbled away and fallen asleep on the couch, passed out cold. Naomi turned up at the house twenty minutes later and said we had to get rid of him. Together we lifted him off the couch and carried him outside. We left him sleeping on the steps of a rehab center after driving him there in the boot of Naomi's car, hoping he would get the hint when he woke up.

But he didn't. Ian turned up the next afternoon, drunk and blazing angry for being left out there in the middle of the night.

Bess was crying because of the continuous banging on the front door, but Naomi was in there with me. She had a baseball bat in one hand, ready to swing it at him if he came in through the window.

We shouted at him. I was crying. I begged him to leave the baby and me alone and go and get some help. Naomi threatened to call the police. He was out there for hours and I didn't think he would ever go but eventually he did.

I never saw him after that. Naomi made me promise I

would call the cops if I ever heard from him again. He'd scared both of us. I just wanted him to get help and leave us alone.

And surprisingly, he did.

He was back, clean and calm, trying to get back on his feet again. I could see why Naomi still hated him. I could also see why Silas thought it was an outrageously stupid idea to let him back into my life. But how could I just abandon the father of my child? Someone who was struggling to piece his life together?

If I rejected him, if I kept his daughter from him—who knew what he would end up doing? I may be driving him toward drugs again. I was trying to help people like him through the agency everyday, how could I deny him help?

But Silas had looked at me like I was committing a crime.

He didn't know Ian.

He didn't know what it was like growing up with an absentee father. I did.

He didn't know what I had been through, and he certainly didn't know what would be best for Bess.

I walked out of the L, wrapping myself up tightly in my coat and scarf as I walked toward the café. I knew I was late. I hadn't even called in. I never did irresponsible things like that. I always tried to maintain the best work ethic on the job, but Silas and Ian had turned everything topsy-turvy.

It physically pained me in my heart, all over my body to realize that Silas was rejecting me. I knew I'd rejected him once already. I'd made the decision of not being with him because Ian was back in our lives again, but that morning was the final straw.

He thought I was being an idiot. He would never see eye

to eye with me. He would never approve of my decision to include Ian.

Was that another one of the things I was going to have to sacrifice for the sake of my daughter's happiness? For the sake of the work I was trying to do in that neighborhood?

Not many people were seeing it that way.

My heart was heavy, my body ached, and I felt like I could go hide under the covers in bed all day. But I had an entire shift to get through. I had money to make and bills to pay. Grieving for a broken heart was not a luxury I could afford.

43

SILAS

I banged the door shut on my way in. I'd forgotten I had company in my apartment.

Sadie came out of the den in her pajamas, with a half-eaten peanut butter and jelly sandwich in one hand. "What are you doing home? It's the middle of the day!"

She had a very good point. I'd missed all my meetings and I was avoiding my calls and emails from the office at that point. After Iris, I tried to go back to work, but I just didn't have it in me to push through it. However, I'd forgotten I had my sister at home too. I pushed past her and headed for the kitchen to pour myself a glass of water.

Sadie followed me. "Silas? What is going on? Is there something wrong between Dad and you? You both were giving each other the dirts the other day."

She watched me pour the water, drink the water, and then I run out of things to engage myself with in order to avoid her questions. "Things are on rocky grounds between us, yeah, kinda, just some business stuff."

Sadie was the only member of the family who had no

idea what Dad and the rest of his crew were involved in. Why Mom had died.

I wanted it to stay that way, to safeguard some of her sanity.

She rubbed my shoulder. "Come on, the two of you have always been so close..."

That was untrue. I was the only one who *tolerated* Dad's bullshit. There was a huge difference.

With a smile, she leaned down trying to get eye contact. "I'm sure you can resolve this. You work together." Why don't you sit down? Let me make you some fluffy eggs. The kind you used to make for me when I was a kid."

I said nothing as I sat down at the breakfast bar. I never told Sadie that those eggs were Mom's staple. I learned to make them like that from her. Sadie never had the pleasure of knowing our mother. The only parent she had ever known was our 'wonderful' father.

I ran a hand through my hair while she started arranging the ingredients on the counter. "Do you want to tell me what's going on between the two of you? Things seemed pretty tense back there that day."

"It's nothing to be worried about, Sades, just let it go," I insisted, but she wasn't about to do that.

She shook her head with a sigh. "What is it with all of you? Why can't you just talk about it? Miles, Alex and you... all the same."

"What do you want me to say?" I snapped as she cracked the eggs in a bowl.

Furling her brow she turned swiftly around. "What is going on with you!"

"It's not about Dad okay? It's about this—woman—a woman I met..." I was dragging the words out of my throat.

Sadie stopped what she was doing and looked up at me with amazed eyes. "What did you just say? Did you just admit that all this grumpiness is over a woman?"

I remained silent while my sister started whipping the eggs, but her eyes were still on me. "Who is she? What's going on? I've never heard you talk about a woman before."

I shook my head. "I don't think we should be talking about her really, because she's not exactly a part of my life anymore."

Sadie cleared her throat. "How long was she a part of your life?"

I shrugged. "Briefly. A few days. It got complicated really quickly."

She crossed her brows and glared at me. "You managed to screw things up with a woman you like within a few days of meeting her?"

Why was I doing that? Why was I talking about Iris? I should have been talking about other things to distract myself from her. "It wasn't a one-sided thing. Things got screwed up on their own. It was circumstantial."

Sadie lifted a brow. "I don't understand..."

"Neither do I," I said.

Sadie sighed. "Getting any information out of you is like prying a tooth out of your mouth. Are you going to tell me anything more than this? Or do you want me to leave you alone, wallowing in your own self-pity?"

I met my sister's eyes and she blinked rapidly, waiting for an answer. The eggs were cooking while she glared me down. "Her ex came back in the picture, just when we started to get comfortable with each other."

She winced. "Shit."

"Yeah, shit is right," I said.

Sadie turned the heat off on the cooktop and scooped the omelet onto a plate. "Has she gone back to him? Did they have a strong history?"

I didn't know why I was telling Sadie everything. Things with Iris were over. "You could say that, I guess. They have a baby together."

Sadie shook her head. "But are they *together* together? Like she chose him over you?"

I groaned, rolling my neck. "She says she has no feelings for him. She doesn't want to be with him, but wants him to be a part of her life because of the kid."

"So why are you moping about?" she asked, a smile on her face.

"It's complicated," I gruffed.

Sadie paused, holding the pan out. "She still wants to keep seeing you right?"

"I don't think so. She doesn't want to confuse the kid."

Sadie pushed the plate of eggs towards me. "Eat that. Those eggs always made me feel better when I was down, remember?"

She had a weak smile on her face. I nodded and cut myself a small piece of the omelet.

"I'm sorry, big brother, that things turned out shitty for you. Was she the first woman you felt anything for?" she asked.

I couldn't reply to that. I couldn't even look her in the eye. I just kept eating like I hadn't heard her say anything.

"I think I know the answer to that question," she said.

Sadie and I sat in silence for a while longer. I finished my eggs and she finished eating her sandwich. After that I said I wanted to be alone for a while and I went to my bedroom and locked myself in there for the rest of the day.

Just like a bratty immature teenager would, not a thirty-five year old chairman of a multi-million dollar real estate company.

44

IRIS

Naomi came over to the apartment for dinner a few nights later. Bess had spent another evening at the park with Ian under my supervision and I could sense a genuine bond forming between father and daughter. Naomi was still staunchly against the choice I made and I was hoping that we could talk openly about it, and hopefully get passed it.

Bess spoke about school and daycare at the dinner table, and also all the fun she'd been having with her dad. Every time she mentioned Ian, I saw Naomi looking away, so I knew I had a lot of work to do.

After dinner we watched an animated movie together with Bess sitting between us with a big bowl of popcorn on her lap. Halfway through the movie though, she fell asleep and Naomi and I helped her into bed.

The bottle of wine was popped open after that and took to our usual spot on the couch. The movie continued in the background while we talked about the agency.

With the help of all the money raised, we were able to

put a down payment on a big building that we would likely own if everything went according to plan.

Naomi and I were both planning on doing a few professional counseling courses in the coming months so we could get certified and prepare ourselves for a more official and well run organization.

After all the work-talk was done, I looked over at her as she sipped on her wine. "I went to see Silas a few days ago so I could explain to him why I'd abruptly cut off ties with him."

She sighed and shook her head. "How did he take it?"

"Not well. Actually, he was fine all through the rest of the story. I tried telling him as much as I could remember from six years ago. But when I got to the part about what happened the night we threw Ian out, he acted out."

Naomi rolled her eyes. "That man clearly has more brain cells than some other people I know."

"Hey!" I snapped.

She looked at me apologetically. "I'm sorry, you know I didn't mean that. I'm just surprised. I thought he was a jackass, and maybe he's not. Maybe I was too quick to judge him and you were right about him all along."

I took a sip of my wine and shrugged. "Well, it doesn't matter. I don't think he's going to be willing to wait till I figure all this out with Ian."

"You wanted him to wait for you?" Naomi asked, sitting up now.

I shrugged. "I didn't say that to him, but the thought crossed my mind. I can't jump into a relationship with him right now because it could confuse Bess...but maybe in a few months..."

Naomi shook her head, giving me a look. "Oh honey, you and I both know it's going to take you more than just a few months to figure this out with Ian. He hasn't even gotten to the point yet where he tells you what he wants."

I groaned, shaking my head. "Why do you have to be like that? Why do you have to immediately assume that he wants something? He's getting what he wants. To spend time with his daughter."

"Because that's how he's always been, Iris! From the start of your relationship. He's been back here, trying to be a couple, trying to have a relationship, when he wanted something from you. Money, sex, more money, a roof over his head!" She was counting them off on her fingers as she went.

I rolled my eyes and looked away.

Naomi's voice grew angrier. "Just tell me honestly, Iris. Do you still have feelings for him?"

When I looked back, I saw that Naomi was standing up. She actually looked angry.

I glared at her. "You can't seriously be asking me that question. I stopped having feelings for that man seven years ago, before I even found out I was pregnant. The only feelings I have for him are pity and a need to help him—just like I want to help every person who walks through the doors of our agency!"

My shoulders were heaving. I was angry too. I couldn't believe she was actually challenging me.

Naomi crossed her arms over her breasts, her glass of wine was dangling from one hand. "I don't believe you. After everything that man has done to you. He could have seriously hurt you. He could have hurt Bess, and now you're giving him another chance because you think he's magically reformed?"

"So, you are saying that none of those people we are

trying to help at the agency are ever going to get better? That they don't deserve a second chance?" I hissed at her.

"Just admit it, Iris. You still have feelings for Ian," she deflected my question.

I stood up angrily. "No. I do not."

"You're lying to yourself!" She squealed.

"I do not have feelings for Ian, Naomi. I have feelings for Silas Denton!" I had screamed the words out.

She stared at me in shock for a few moments before she saw the tears that were beginning to roll down my cheeks.

"Oh, honey, I'm sorry..." She threw her arms open and came toward me.

I let her hold me in her arms. "I have feelings for Silas and I keep pushing him away, and now he's pushing me away too. I don't know what to do."

Naomi patted my back and held me tightly. "You're allowed to cry, Iris, you're allowed to hurt. Just let it out."

I couldn't make the tears stop. I didn't even realize I was capable of crying like that anymore.

45

SILAS

I met this girl, I thought her name was Claire. I met her at the bar I usually went for a drink at on Friday nights. I'd been working late at the office and I walked over to the bar and ordered a few whiskeys to get my mind off everything I felt was going wrong in my life.

Claire was sitting beside me and she started a conversation I wasn't initially interested in.

Then I noticed her long dark hair and green eyes. She was wearing a short shiny looking cocktail dress that I couldn't imagine was to Iris' taste, but it looked smashing on Claire's curvaceous body. While she spoke and laughed, I ordered a few more drinks and pictured Iris sitting there instead.

We'd never actually been on a real date together. The dinner at Boheme was before either of us admitted we wanted something real.

I tried to imagine what it would feel like if Claire was Iris and we were just sharing a drink together at a bar. No baggage, no complications, no history—just two people enjoying each other's company because they were attracted to each other.

It had been several days since I last saw her, but she was still constantly on my mind.

Claire leaned in to me and ran her fingers up and down the length of my arm. "You know you're a really good listener."

She was close enough for her lips to make contact with my ear.

I couldn't remember how I would have reacted to that situation before Iris came into my life, when I wasn't fantasizing about a woman I couldn't actually have.

"Let's get outta here," I declared and emptied the whisky down my throat.

Claire didn't need to be coaxed. She jumped off her chair and weaved her arm into mine as we walked out of the bar together.

"I've told you so much about me, but you've told me nothing about you—Silas Denton," she said with a giggle.

I was in no condition to drive. I'd had too much to drink already, though I was still thirsty. We stopped a cab and got in.

"There isn't much to know about me," I replied to her statement.

"Everyone has a story, and you definitely look like a man with a story," she said.

My vision was blurring at that point. Sometimes I imagined Iris there instead of Claire, and sometimes I could see the stark differences on that woman's face, and it made me feel sick.

It was too late at that point, even though I'd changed my mind. We were already at my apartment building and she was following me out of the cab.

I swayed on my feet and Claire giggled, jumping for my arm and leading me into the lobby.

"Which floor?" she asked as we headed unsteadily for the elevator.

"Penthouse," I replied and she looked impressed.

"Look, see the thing is, Claire...I'm not sure I was thinking this through before." I tried to make her see.

Usually, it was no problem for me to set the record straight and make my intentions clear, but I was sensing that I might have had a little too much to drink that night and I was also starting to feel physically weak.

"You don't have to worry about that, Silas. I'll do all the work," she said huskily.

Claire drew closer to me as the elevator zoomed up. She threw her arms around me and I could feel her pressing into my body, rubbing herself on me.

I found the strength to forcibly peel her off me and the elevator doors pinged open.

"Okay, I'm not making myself totally clear here. This is a mistake. I shouldn't have invited you back here," I said as I sliced my card key into the slot and the front door unlocked.

Claire was still smiling. She wasn't actually taking my protest too seriously.

"Don't be silly..." she purred.

I kicked the front door open with my foot and stumbled in. She followed me in before I could stop her. I was backing away from her while she tried to get close to me. It wasn't until Sadie turned up in the hallway that Claire actually stopped in her tracks.

"Hey, everything okay here?" Sadie asked.

Claire glared angrily at her first.

"You have another girl in your apartment?" she hissed, whipping around to me.

I found a smile tugging the corners of my lips. This wasn't necessarily a funny situation, but I'd had too much to drink and had no control over my reactions anymore.

"I'm his sister!" Sadie snapped, crossing her arms over her chest.

Claire rolled her eyes.

"What is going on, Silas?" she asked.

I shrugged.

"I think my brother is drunk and he might have given you the wrong impression about what he wants right now." Sadie was doing all the talking for me.

Suddenly, I'd turned into a person who couldn't even take care of himself.

Claire glared at me some more and I continued to smile at her.

"I think you should leave. That would be for the best," Sadie insisted.

When I didn't try and stop her, Claire didn't seem to have any other choice but to follow Sadie to the door.

"Call me?" she murmured and I saluted her.

Sadie shut the door and turned to me with her nostrils flared. "What the fuck are you actually doing, Silas?"

I was expecting a scolding so I'd already started to walk away but she was following me to my bedroom door.

"You think you're going to be able to get over her by bringing some other girl over? Were you even going to actually sleep with her?" Sadie asked.

I walked into my bedroom.

"You've had too much to drink. You're going to seriously hurt yourself if you don't stop now! Silas!"

I shut the door in her face.

IRIS

I'd spent last night crying, and poor Naomi had spent it trying to console me. I knew she felt partially responsible for me breaking down, because she kept pushing me about Ian. However, she wasn't expecting me to break down over Silas. Maybe because I hadn't shown to her or anybody else what I was really feeling. Our relationship had been so short lived.

We eventually fell asleep in the living room. Me on the couch and Naomi on the rug on the floor. We'd polished off two bottles of wine between us and when I woke up the next morning, I had a raging throbbing headache.

Thankfully, it was a Saturday and I was even more grateful that Bess wasn't up to see us like that. I dragged myself off the couch and went into the kitchen to get the coffee started.

I didn't have to go to the café till later in the day and Sarah and some volunteers that were going to cover for me later at the agency, so I had a relatively easy day. That meant I could nurse my hell fire hangover without too much chaos around me.

I smiled looking down at Naomi sleeping on the floor in the fetal position. I caught sight of myself in a mirror while I made the coffee and it shocked me. My face was covered in smudged makeup from all the crying I had done. My hair and clothes were a mess. My mouth was stained from the wine we'd been drinking—I definitely needed to jump in the shower before Bess saw me like that.

I had been nothing but a responsible mother to her for her entire little life, and I didn't want to start proving to be otherwise.

While I was brewing the coffee, I saw a letter being popped in under the front door. At first, I figured I'd pick it up later, but then I thought it was odd to have a letter be delivered on a Saturday morning, so I decided to check it out.

I picked it off the floor and saw that the envelope just had my name on it, not even the address. Clearly, it had been delivered personally by hand.

I went over to the window and peeped out through the curtains. I couldn't see anybody on the street below who I recognized. Who would have dropped off a letter at my apartment?

I proceeded to rip the envelope open and pull the pages out.

They looked like official letters. Then I focused and saw that the letters were from some kind of a legal office. My eyes scanned the words quickly, trying to make sense of all the things I was reading. Then the pages fell on the floor and I screamed as loud as I could.

∼

"Here you go," Naomi handed me my mug of coffee.

I was sitting on the couch with a blanket around my shoulders and still I was shivering. I had never felt that cold before in my life.

"Where is Bess?" I asked my best friend.

She was crouched down in front of me with her hands on my knees. "I've made sure she's in her room, she's drawing and playing with her toys. I've told her you and I need to have a little grown-up chat without her. She's going to stay in her room."

The pages from the envelope were still lying on the floor near the window where I'd left them. I was so afraid of them that I hadn't let Naomi touch them yet. "Can you tell me what was in the letter? You said it's a legal notice. A legal notice from Ian..."

I wiped my cheeks with my hand. They were still damp. I couldn't stop crying or shivering. I felt like I was falling apart. I'd never felt that afraid about anything, not even four years ago when I thought Ian was going to kill me.

"He wants full custody of Bessy," I murmured.

Naomi was silent for a few moments. She rubbed my knees but I could sense she was finding it hard to believe too.

"Okay...alright...well, he can want whatever he wants, doesn't mean he's actually going to get it. We're going to fight this thing."

I sniffled, looking away from her. "They're rich, Naomi. His family is rich. They can afford the best lawyers in the city, and I know how important family and bloodline and all that is to them. They're going to do everything they can to take what is theirs, and they believe that Bess is theirs."

I was shaking again and she got up to sit beside me on the couch and rub my shoulders. "We can get lawyers too..."

"They're going to do everything they can to turn me into this monster. They know I'll never be able to afford to keep up a legal battle for too long. I live on the Southside, I have no money, no savings, my entire family has a history of drug abuse..."

"But *you* don't, Iris. You've been clean all your life and Ian hasn't."

"You think it'll be that easy to prove? You think they can't plant false evidence? Ian's family is not going to shy away from playing dirty if they think it'll get them what they want, and they want Bess."

Naomi stared back at me with worried eyes.

I burst into tears again, trembling with terror. I'd never considered the possibility...that I could ever come close to losing my baby girl. I just wished Silas was holding me. That he had his arms around me telling me everything was going to be fine. He would have known how to make me feel safe again, but I couldn't go to him, not after the way I'd already turned him away.

47

SILAS

When I woke up the next day, I was surprised to find myself in my own bed. My head felt like it was being ripped open and my lips were chapped and dry. I could smell the alcohol sweat on my sheets. Everything stank of the night before.

It could have been morning or it could have been the afternoon. I dragged myself out of bed, barely being able to walk to the bathroom. I saw myself in the mirror, looking like a dark shadow of my previous self.

I needed a shave and a shower.

I spent too long doing both. It felt like my limbs were refusing to function on their own. The headache was persistent, and felt like it was only getting worse. I needed to go to work, I'd missed too many days at the office already—although I had no idea how I would get any work done in that state.

I put on fresh clothes after the shower and stripped the bed linen. I hoped Sadie wasn't still at the apartment. The last thing I wanted was to face my sister and be reminded of my actions from the previous night.

I stepped out of my room hesitantly, but immediately the smell of coffee hit my nostrils and I felt awake.

"Silas?" It was Sadie's voice.

She appeared at the door of the den with her hands on her hips. "You're alive!"

"I need coffee," I groaned.

"There's coffee in here, and some food, come in," she said, indicating the den.

I stood for a moment, debating whether to follow her in or not. I wasn't exactly in the mood for much talking, but it didn't seem like Sadie was going to let it drop either.

I had no choice but to follow her in, and I found our father sitting there on my couch, sipping coffee from a cup. I glared at Sadie who shrugged. I knew she meant well. She didn't want us to argue, even though she didn't know the real reason why we had a falling out—so really, it wasn't her fault.

"Good morning, son. Sadie tells me you had a long night," Dad said with a smile on his face, like he enjoyed seeing me in pain.

I looked at my sister with narrowed eyes. "Give us some time alone, Sades."

She glanced at Dad, then at me again, and nodded. "I'm going to go for my salon appointment now. See you soon. Bye Daddy."

"What are you doing here, Dad?" I asked, turning to him as soon as Sadie had left the room. As if the morning wasn't going badly enough already.

"I came to talk to you, to finally put all this animosity to rest," he replied.

"What do you think is really going on between us, Dad?" I asked him, walking over to the coffee table so I could pour some coffee from the pot into a cup for myself.

Sadie had done good. I heard Dad sigh.

There were some cookies on a plate. I took two and walked away from the couch.

My father smacked his lips together, looking as arrogant as ever. "It seems like I've hurt your feelings. Maybe I embarrassed you by sending you to that fundraiser because that charity refused to take the check once they saw our name on it. Which I personally think is ridiculous."

I had walked over to the glass wall, looking out at Chicago's busy Saturday bustling life.

I took a bite of the cookie. "I don't think you ever really understood why Alex and Miles tried to get as far away from you as they could, did you? Do you even know why Mom did what she did?"

"Don't you dare bring her into this!" His voice had changed.

I had upset him. He didn't like to talk about her. I could see his reflection in the glass. He was glaring at me.

I continued, not giving a damn about his feelings. "She is in the middle of all this, Dad. If it wasn't for her, we'd still be on the Southside. You'd still be doing the same work. Bloodying our hands."

He got off the couch and strode toward me. "I gave you what you wanted. I shut it down. I moved here. I go to work in that metal fucking tower and attend fucking board meetings and wear a suit!"

I turned to him slowly seeing how red his face had turned. His eyes were popping out with rage. "And the only reason you're doing any of those things is because you're afraid one of us will go to the cops with evidence against you. Against our own father. Not because you actually wanted to shut down the business or change your life."

"Fuck you, son," Dad growled.

I wasn't surprised. He'd grown up on the Southside, he'd grown up rough. He didn't really give a shit about his kids. All he'd ever really cared about was the business and Mom, now they were both gone.

"You want to keep me from going to the cops about you? Make a real fucking effort to atone your sins," I replied.

"You heard me? Fuck you!" He continued.

I drank my coffee and took another bite of the cookie. My hangover had gone nowhere, but it felt good to finally tell my father what I thought of him. He whipped away from me and stormed out of the den. I heard the front door open and shut. He was gone.

I plopped down on the couch. How long was I going to carry the guilt and the burden for my family? My father was never going to repent for his actions. With my siblings out of the picture, it would always have to be me.

Me trying to make our business clean.

Me donating to the right charities.

Me feeling the guilt all my life because the money and riches we had were all tainted.

48

IRIS

I had to take a few hours off my shift at the café to make my way there. I knew my increasing absence and delays at the cafe were going to start being noticed soon, but I couldn't help it. Everything that was going on, it was a problem that needed to be dealt with right away.

I could have stayed home and cried some more, or I could do something about it.

There was no way I would let Ian take Bess away from me. Over my dead body.

I knew the address to his family home even though he'd never taken me there for a visit before. I rapped loudly on the door till someone opened. She appeared to be a housekeeper or a maid of some sort.

"Yes?" she sounded bored.

"I'm here to speak to Ian. Where is he?" I spat at her, trying to peep into the house.

From everything I'd seen of the house yet, his people were loaded.

When Ian and I first met, he couldn't stop talking about

how terrible and money-minded his family was. How there was no affection between them and he was so glad to be finally rid of them so he could have a normal life. It was disgusting to think that he'd scurried back to them.

"Who are you?" the woman asked and I didn't want to waste any more time.

"Ian!" I screamed. Loud enough for anyone in the house to hear. "Ian!"

I screamed again till I heard the sound of shuffling feet behind the woman who looked a little taken aback now.

Ian pushed the woman aside and came charging toward me. It was late morning and it seemed like he'd been sleeping.

"What the fuck are you doing, Iris?" He growled and slammed the front door shut behind him.

I took a step back, glaring at him. I was well covered up in warm clothing but he was in his pajamas, his hair was all ruffled and it looked like he had a sudden rude awakening from his sleep.

"What do you think I'm doing, Ian? I'm here to warn you to back off."

He ran a hand through his hair and shrugged. "It's done, Iris. They've got our family lawyers on the case. My mother didn't know I had a kid, not till three months ago when I finally told her and now, they're obsessed with the thought of bringing a grandchild home. Especially since my sister can't have kids."

I was beside myself. "I thought you came to see Bess because you actually cared about her. I thought you wanted to be a real dad to her!"

He yawned. "I do and I'm going to be. I wasn't lying when I said I'm clean now. I'm ready to be a father now."

I peered into Ian's eyes, hoping he had some shred of

feeling left in him. "You can still be a father, Ian. I'm not going to stop you. I opened up our lives to you, despite everything. I want what is best for her, but not like this. Not while we're in the middle of a legal battle!"

"My family will be able to provide a much better life for her than you will."

It wasn't working. He wasn't going to see reason. "You all want to take an innocent six year old girl away from her mother? You were an addict, Ian. You were dangerous and violent and disgusting. You didn't give a shit about her four years ago when I threw you out of our home because you nearly choked me to death!"

I was screaming at that point. Ian looked guiltily about him, probably hoping that nobody else could hear me screaming—but he didn't tell me to shut up either. "You have no proof."

I crossed my arms. "Naomi will be my witness."

He licked his lips and looked at me with an expressionless face. "And my family has an outstanding record of social service and goodwill in the community. We are rich. We entertain judges and prosecutors for dinner over the weekend. My family has too many personal connections to make this happen for us."

My anger was quickly turning to a sense of loss. I could feel the tears threatening to burst.

Ian drew in a deep breath and crossed his arms over his chest. "Just give up quietly, Iris. Don't make a fuss and we can come to some sort of an arrangement to your benefit. I'm sure I can convince my folks into letting you visit Bess a few times a month."

"How could you..." I murmured the words as I felt the Earth shake under my feet.

Ian shrugged. For a moment he actually looked apologetic. "She belongs to us, Iris. She's our flesh and blood. If you don't fight us now, they'll be willing to compensate you for the past six years—you know, money-wise."

I whipped away from him just as the tears started to roll down my cheeks. I didn't want him to see me cry. I stuffed my hands in the pockets of my jacket and hurried down the driveway.

How could he even say those things? He saw us together. He saw how much I loved my daughter, the bond we shared, how much we cared for each other. How could he, as a father, even dream of snatching her away from me? After I gave him a second chance?

Naomi and Silas were right...

I turned the corner from the house and broke down in tears. I couldn't go back to the cafe like that. I didn't know how I could even face the day. I didn't even know how to face Bess without crying. I was going to fight this till my last breath. I would rather die than have my daughter taken away from me.

49

SILAS

I heard the intercom ringing in the other room but I didn't bother to go get it. I didn't even want to open the door when the bell rang.

I'd been sitting in the den for some time after Dad left, drinking glass after glass of water to rehydrate myself. The headache was slowly beginning to soften its pumping blows, and even though I didn't feel a hundred percent yet, I decided I was going to get myself ready to go to the office after lunch hour.

I needed to find a way to get myself back to work, back to my old routine. It was the life I knew, what I did best.

But the bell rang again and I figured it was Sadie who'd forgotten her keycard.

I went to the door feeling exhausted and opened it. I found Iris on the other side.

"I didn't know if you'd be at home or the office," she said.

There was something strange about her voice. I could sense she was not completely herself.

Why was it, that despite how badly our last meetings ended, we always wound up drifting to each other? That time I was sure I wouldn't see her again. I figured I'd hurt her sentiments enough. But there she was, standing at my door, trying her best to hold her head up high.

"You found me," I said stepping to the side so she could come in.

My body did the same thing it always did when my eyes fell on Iris. It stiffened up with desire, no matter how heavy my hangover was. Just being in her presence made me feel like I was fully recovered again.

I got a whiff of her shampoo when she drifted past me, hurrying down the hallway, heading straight for the den. She'd been there once before but it seemed like she knew my apartment inside out. That made me feel strangely good.

I followed her in.

"Coffee?" I offered.

It seemed like she was there for a very particular reason. Like she had something important to say. But I didn't want her to say it yet, just so that maybe we could lengthen her stay there.

"I'm fine, thanks. Aren't you going to ask me what I'm doing here?" she asked.

I watched her pace around the room. Up and down the width of my large white rug, with her arms crossed over her breasts. She'd taken her scarf and jacket off. Underneath, she was wearing a t-shirt that stretched tightly over her voluptuous breasts and hips. Her jeans were equally tight over her butt. I tried not to concentrate so hard on her body, but it was difficult not to when she was dangling herself like that in front of me.

"I figured you'd tell me eventually," I said and sat down on the couch.

But Iris was not about to sit down it seemed. She kept pacing, in a rush. It was obvious that she had a lot on her mind. "The last time we saw each other, Silas, I promised myself that we couldn't see each other anymore. I mean, you made it so obvious that you didn't want to have anything to do with me."

"And you made it pretty clear that there is no space for me in your or Bess'," I said.

Iris snorted sarcastically at that, but I had no idea why. Like mentioning her daughter's name was funny somehow.

"Isn't that what you said? That you would rather deal with your ex right now than deal with me?" I urged her.

Iris rolled her eyes and then resumed her pacing. She was shaking her head in silence and I had no idea what the fuck was going on anymore.

"Okay, Iris, I'll bite. Why are you here? Why are we still talking about this? Why aren't we moving on from this yet?" I asked.

She came to a stop in front of me. "I'm here because I just need one moment, just some time when I don't have to think. When I can just blank myself out, forget everything else and just focus on feeling good."

Her eyes drooped and became heavy. I remained sitting on the couch as she walked slowly toward me, taking one step at a time. I wasn't entirely sure yet but I thought I understood what she was trying to get at—she wanted a quickie.

"Iris, I'm really not sure this is a good idea for us," I protested.

Of course, there was nothing else I wanted more than her body. I'd been thinking about it every minute of every hour since I first met her. But if we did it, there was no going back. How was I going to forget about her after that?

Iris kept moving toward me, her hips swaying, her eyes

glazed over. She was doing the thing she was talking about —allowing her mind to just go blank.

"This is what we're good for together, Silas. Meaningless, great sex," she whispered hoarsely and before I could stop her, she was rolling her t-shirt up over her head and throwing it to the floor.

She undid her jeans and pushed them down her legs, stepping out of them. Iris was standing directly over me in nothing but her sleek chocolate colored lace bra and panties.

"What do you want, Silas?"

I looked up at her feeling like a defeated man. I knew my cock was tenting my jeans. I clenched my jaw, giving it one last-ditched attempt at resisting.

She was too powerful. I reached up and grabbed her hand, pulling her down into my lap. I could never resist her.

50

IRIS

I was on Silas' lap, grinding against his hard throbbing cock. His arms were around me, his hands on my breasts as our lips met, our mouths colliding. I could taste him, his tongue diving deep into my mouth. Tenderly, he started to push down my bra so my breasts bounced from their restraints.

He squeezed my nipples and I cried out with joy.

My panties were wet, brushing against his erect cock. I moved my hands down to his pants, pulling down the zip, reaching for it. I could feel it getting bigger in my hand and I rolled my hips wilder.

His fingers were all over me, feeling my breasts and moving down to my hips, then my butt, squeezing every inch of my skin.

When his fingers found my pussy, I cried out again, pulling my mouth away from him.

"Silas..." I hissed his name and he peered into my eyes.

He wrapped his arms around me and still holding me tight, he lifted me off the couch, standing up. I gasped and wrapped my legs around him. Where was he taking me?

I was breathless. He walked down the hall corridor and kicked open the bedroom door. His bedroom. There were no sheets, just a mattress...I almost laughed out loud because of how strange the bed looked in such a perfectly luxurious room.

He lowered me down and my back met the springy soft mattress.

I watched as he started undressing himself. First his t-shirt, then his jeans. He wasn't wearing any underwear, but that wasn't a surprise. His cock stood erect between his muscular thighs. His body was perfectly chiseled. He was the sexiest man I'd ever met, and it was still crazy to me that he wanted me just as badly.

Silas threw himself at me, covering me with his enormous and strong body. I felt like I was crushed under him and nothing in my life felt that good. Being enveloped by him, being possessed by him.

He rolled down my panties, sliding our naked bodies together. I could feel his cock stroking against my belly as he kissed my neck.

I held on to his solid arms, digging my nails into his bulging muscles. We started moving together, rubbing against each other. Suddenly he grabbed my wrists and pinned them to the bed.

"Stay still woman," he growled as I nearly choked with want.

He wedged himself between my legs and started lowering himself down the bed, his mouth hovering over my pussy. I felt his hot breath, his delicious tongue, and I screamed with pleasure as he started licking.

It felt beyond amazing. I clutched his hair, holding on to it like reigns on a horse while he licked and stroked my pussy dry, plunging his tongue in until I gave up. I was coming. My body seemed to somersault as I lay there on the bed. I pressed my eyes closed and my toes curled.

Silas didn't stop till I was done, so out of breath that I couldn't even tell him how amazing it was. I looked down between my legs and found Silas looking up at me with a crooked smile on his face. He was wiping his lips with the back of his hand.

"My turn," he said huskily as he rose up and reached for the bedside table where he clearly kept his condoms.

I watched him with admiration as he put it on. His big hulking mass of solid muscle, so unbelievably handsome... and possessing that secret ability to make a woman feel safe and cared for in his presence. No matter what bad-boy player impression Silas first made, that was the core of him. I blinked, trying to push the thoughts away.

I was there for a good time. For the sex. That is what we'd signed up for. No feelings anymore.

Silas climbed on top of me, his eyes flitting over my outstretched body and I bit down on my lip as he lowered himself down.

I felt his cock thrust in, deep and fitting tight in my pussy. It felt so good. It felt like I was coming home. Like his cock had belonged inside me all along.

I reached out and wrapped my arms around him, scratching his back with my nails as he started pumping. He moved in and out. Our bodies danced in a synchronic motions, our moans echoing around us.

The orgasm began to rise up inside of me all over again. I wanted to feel the pleasure and the vibration of it. Silas groaned and I moaned along with him as we both erupted simultaneously.

We came, crying out and holding each other tight, rocking together while his thrusts became quicker and then slowly started to subside. The bed was shaking the room seemed to spin around us. It was the best sex I had ever had. I would never be able to forget the experience. Silas Denton had made me forget...

After our orgasms subsided, while we were still breathing hard, he rolled over beside me, staring up at the ceiling. I wished I knew what he was thinking of me, and I wished I could tell him what was going on in my life.

I couldn't be honest with him, but I didn't want him involved. I needed to do it on my own, like I'd done everything else in my life. I came there so I could hopefully feel good for just a split second, to stop the swarm of thoughts and rage in my mind. That had definitely been successful.

Silas was never a man to disappoint.

But very soon, it was going to be time for me to go.

51

SILAS

Iris was the first one to sit up in bed. She was the one who was in a hurry to go.

I watched as she scouted around the bedroom for her lingerie and started putting it back on. She kept her back turned to me so I couldn't see her face. But she didn't have to tell me anything else for me to know that there was something critical on her mind. Something was going on in her life she wasn't telling me about.

My best guess was this was about her ex.

"I'll get them," I said, as she looked around for her clothes. I knew they were in the den. I put on my jeans first and stepped out of the room.

Thankfully, Sadie wasn't back yet.

When I returned, Iris was sitting on the edge of the bed, with her back straight and her face sullen. I wanted to tell her how beautiful she looked, how much I wanted to work everything out.

There was no denying that she was my soulmate. Losing her had made my soul hurt in a way it had never hurt before.

I handed over her jeans, t-shirt, jacket and her scarf, all of which she quickly put on.

"So why exactly did you want to switch yourself off today?" I asked.

I'd stuck my hands in the pockets of my jeans and I was leaning against the dresser in my room, watching Iris dress. She avoided my eyes and flipped her thick lustrous dark hair to the other side.

"Just with everything going on in my life, you know, I needed a break. That was all," she replied.

I could hear it in her voice, there was something else going on.

"How is Bess?" I asked.

She glanced up at me and I saw a sudden rage in her eyes. For the second time that day, she had reacted strangely to the mention of her daughter.

"Is everything okay with her? You seem unwilling to talk about her," I said.

I heard her take in a deep breath. "There is nothing to talk about."

"About the most important person in your life, Iris? I find that hard to believe."

She must have heard the seriousness in my voice because she jerked her head up to look at me. Her lips were pursed tightly closed with that fire in her eyes again. She was fully dressed but still sitting on my bed.

"I don't *want* to talk about her," she said.

I narrowed my eyes. So, this was the sore point? Something was going on with Bess. Just that realization was enough to have me worried.

I walked up closer to her, standing over her with my shoulders squared. "Iris, I want you to tell me what is going on with Bess, right now."

She licked her lips and weaved her fingers through her hair and shook it out. "Why do you want to know anything, Silas? None of this concerns you. I came here for a very specific thing. It seems like we are both satisfied with it and now it's over."

"Iris, what is going on with Bess? Did that bastard do anything to her?" I growled.

There was a flash of fear in her eyes for a moment, or was it sadness?

She stood up and tried to brush past me.

"I have to go," she murmured.

I grabbed her by her shoulders, holding her in place. "Iris, tell me now so I can help you."

She pulled herself away from me, stepping back. "I don't need your help. Nobody can help me with this. I just need to fight my way through this just like with everything else."

Her cheeks were flushed, tears were brimming in her eyes. I could see her struggling to hold back her tears.

"Is Bess okay?" I asked in a quieter voice.

"She's fine, she's with Naomi right now," she replied and before the tears could roll down her cheeks, she brushed them away with her hands. "I just need to find a solution and I *will* find a solution."

"To what?" I asked.

She turned and walked to my bedroom door. "Ian threatened me with full custody for Bess. He has his family's support. They're loaded. They can get their lawyers to prove lies against me if they have to."

For a moment I thought I didn't hear her correctly. Her ex-addict, ex-boyfriend, father of her child, was now threatening to sue her for full custody of their daughter?

"Iris..." I called out her name.

She whipped around to face me, with her back against the door.

"I'll be fine, Silas. I just needed to clear my head." There was a soft grin on her face now, which was forced and fake. "So, thanks for that."

She opened the bedroom door and I followed her out. She was running down the corridor when the front door of the apartment opened and Sadie stepped in.

Iris stopped in her tracks.

"Oh!" she exclaimed, and Sadie left the door open.

"Oh?" My sister said and looked at me over Iris' shoulder.

Iris didn't even turn to look at me, she just kept walking, charging right out through the door. The elevator was waiting for her and she jumped in before I could get to her.

The doors started to slide close, and she glared directly at me. "Leave me alone, Silas."

It came out as an exhaustive plea, like she just couldn't deal with anything else. So, I didn't jump in. I gave her what she was asking for and I kept my distance.

The doors closed and I watched the digital numbers change quickly as the elevator shot down.

"Was that her?" I heard Sadie's voice behind me at the door.

I turned around to face her and all I could do was just shut my eyes in defeat.

52

IRIS

Naomi and Bess were home together watching cartoons. I tried to not bang the door shut when I came in but Bess knew something was wrong. I'd been behaving strangely all morning.

She came running to me and I lifted her up in my arms. It was hard even holding her without falling apart. I buried my nose in her soft cake-smelling hair. She was my baby, my angel, the best thing that had happened to me in my life. My inspiration to live better.

I spun her around and she held me tightly.

"Are you okay, Mommy?" she asked.

I peered into her eyes fondly. She could see I'd been crying. "I'll be fine, sweetheart. I'm just not feeling too well today."

But she wasn't willing to let me go, she held on to my little finger tightly. "Maybe we can make chicken soup, like you make me when I'm feeling sick?"

I kissed the top of her head lovingly.

Naomi was watching us, I could tell she was distressed too.

"Maybe later, that's a good idea honey," I said.

"Are you going to work?" Bess asked.

"I don't think so. I'm not well and I'd rather spend my time with you. Does that sound okay?" I tried to smile and she nodded.

I wasn't willing to let go of her yet either. I held her by her tiny precious arms and looked into her face. The face I'd nurtured and looked after.

I crouched down in front of her. "Baby, I want you to know that no matter what happens, I will never let anything bad ever happen to you. Do you trust me?"

Bess looked confused at first but then she nodded her head. "Yes, Mommy, I trust you."

I kissed her again and hugged her tightly. I felt like I was going to cry. Where was I going to find the money for the lawyers we'd need? What if Ian wasn't lying about all the judges and prosecutors they had in their pockets? I didn't stand a chance against any of it.

But Bess didn't need to know about all of that. I was going to have to do everything I could to protect her. The last thing she needed to know was that her parents were fighting over her. That her father was trying to take her away from me.

"Okay, sweetie, why don't you go watch TV and maybe we could do something fun together later?" I suggested.

Bess nodded and went back to the couch. Naomi came over so we could talk.

"I'm sorry, I'm sure you have a million other things to do," I apologized.

She rolled her eyes. "Nothing is more important right now than making sure that Bess is exactly where she belongs. So, did you get to speak to Ian?"

We walked to the kitchen to get out of Bess' earshot. "He

basically told me there is nothing I can do or say to convince him and his family to drop the case. They are most definitely going ahead with it. They are coming after Bess and me."

Naomi clenched her fists in anger. She looked about ready to punch something. "I cannot believe he even thinks for a moment that he has any right over that kid!"

"It doesn't matter. He said his family knows people, like judges and lawyers and people like that. Nothing is stopping them from getting what they want. I'm toast."

I rubbed my fingers on my temples feeling another headache coming on.

"We'll raise the money for the legal fees somehow." It was Naomi's turn to pace around the kitchen now.

"I went to see Silas," I said and she stopped in her tracks.

"Oh my God! That is a brilliant idea. Did you tell him everything? Did you ask him for help?" She jumped at me.

I shook my head. "I didn't go to him for help, Naomi. I went to him because I needed comforting. I just needed to get away from all this for some time."

Naomi looked at me confusedly, her face was pinched. "You went to him for sex? You couldn't ask him for his help at the same time?"

"I don't need his help," I barked.

Naomi scoffed. "Are you serious?"

"I can do this. Like you said, we'll raise the money. I'll find the money. I'll start an online petition. I'll go to the newspapers if I have to. I'm not going to shy away from getting dirty!"

Naomi shook her head. "And what do you think that is going to do to Bess? How long is this going to go on for? And what if Ian's family wins in the end? What happens to you and her then?"

My lips were quivering but I tried to keep it together. "That is not going to happen. I am not going to lose my daughter."

Naomi put her hand on my arm. "Don't miss this opportunity to ask for help, Iris, just because of your stubbornness."

I pushed past her and ran out of the kitchen and to my bedroom. I shut the door behind me and collapsed on the floor. I was crying. I was howling in pain because I couldn't imagine a life without Bess. Where was I supposed to find the strength to do anything?

Was Naomi right? Should I have asked Silas for his help?

What kind of person would that make me? I couldn't do that. I couldn't stoop so low. Bess wouldn't want me to...

I covered my face with my hands and continued to cry because I couldn't think of a way out of it.

53

SILAS

I got off the call with Roger Mortimer in my office. It was a good call, perfectly productive. He was going to get the ball rolling first thing Monday morning. Roger Mortimer didn't usually receive business calls on a Sunday morning but when he heard it was Silas Denton on the line, he got out of his hot tub and took the call.

It wasn't often that I took pride in my family name, and I most certainly didn't name-drop on a regular basis, but today I was pleased with myself. And now I had some other business to attend to.

I'd left a voice message on Ian Sheffield's phone which I was guessing he'd received, based on the text message I got back from him.

I walked out of my office, it was completely empty. No Lena, no receptionists or other secretaries scurrying about, trying to get me into meetings. I'd spent the morning working on the problem until I found a solution. And it was done.

I walked out of my office building and got in my Cadillac. I was meeting Ian Sheffield at an upscale cocktail bar. I couldn't wait to see that fucker's face.

He'd arrived there already, dressed for a business meeting. I recognized him because of the photographs I'd scoured of him online. The Sheffield family was moderately well known around Chicago. His grandfather had started a cement company seventy years before and the business had boomed. Now the rest of the family was living off the success. Ian believed he was making good contacts.

I walked up to the bar and he stood up from the leather stool.

"Mr. Denton!" He exclaimed and extended his hand.

"Please, have a seat," I said and we both sat down.

"What are you having?" he asked and I looked at the bartender and ordered a Whisky Sour for myself.

"I was surprised to hear from you, but then my brother in law informed me that people on our side have been trying to get a meeting with you or your father for months. It would be our pleasure to do business with you." To his credit, Ian was aptly excited.

He could barely sit still on his chair. Having been an ex-drug addict who had spent some time on the Southside, meant that he had to have been familiar with my family and its reputation—but it didn't seem to bother him.

"I understand that you've been out of the family business for a few years?" I asked.

He tugged at his collar nervously and chuckled. "Yeah, you could say that. I was young, you know? The usual. Thought I'd give a few other things a shot. But I'm back now. My dad and brother-in-law are filling me in on the business. In fact, they just informed me about the latest deal you and your company have struck with this brand new building project."

Ian was working overtime to please me. I could sense it about him. I still couldn't believe it was that guy, that fucking loser who was trying to take Bess away from Iris.

"Yeah, the building project, sure, and there's another new project I've recently taken on which I wanted to acquaint you and your family with," I said.

Ian shifted enthusiastically in his seat. "I'm all ears."

I could sense myself beginning to smile already.

"Have you heard of Roger Mortimer? The lawyer? I've engaged him and his office's services this morning to begin an investigative case against your family... and *you* specifically."

Ian looked confused at first and then I could see his face starting to turn red and contort.

"When he heard your name, he said his team will not need more than one week to dig up all the material they will require to file at least a dozen criminal charges against your family... and you personally."

Ian put his cocktail glass down.

"What are you talking about?" he asked.

His enforced good manners were beginning to weaken.

"Does that sound about right?" I asked.

"What the fuck is this? You threatening my family for something?"

I got off my stool so I could tower over him. "If you think you can threaten Iris Neilson and take her daughter away with a few false accusations, you're playing a children's game with me. I'm going to bury you and your family under so many criminal charges for the next five decades that you'll have to flee the country and change your names."

I inched closer and closer to him. Ian's eyes had grown larger in his head. Did he look like he was about to cry?

"I'm sure you've heard of us. The Dentons. You know exactly what we are capable of."

Ian gulped and stumbled off his stool. He held his hands up in the air. "Okay, okay, I'll talk to my family. I'll tell them to back off. It's not like I wanted the kid in the first place."

I continued to follow him while he backed away from me.

"Iris and Bess never hear another peep from anybody from the Sheffield family or Roger Mortimer's office files the charges against you. I'm not ever calling the dogs off you."

Ian turned on his heels and ran out of the bar. I could have followed him. I could have driven my knuckles into his nose like I really wanted to do, but that would make me no better than my dad or one of his goons.

I returned to the counter and finished the remaining Whisky Sour and then ordered another one.

If that was the effect Iris' tear brimmed eyes had on me, I was afraid of getting to know what else I was capable of doing to keep her safe and happy.

54

IRIS

Three days went by since I received the first legal letters from the Sheffield family and not a peep. Then another week went by and still, I hadn't heard from them. I hadn't received a call or a text from Ian either. I didn't want to jinx it, but it was starting to feel like they had forgotten that they'd threatened to take Bess away.

I was at the agency with Naomi the next Saturday, while one of the volunteers was watching Bess and a few other kids whose mothers were with us for counseling. Over the course of that week, I'd been bringing Bess with me to the agency because I wanted to keep her close to me. I would have brought her to the café too if I could. I didn't want to take my eyes off her for even a minute. I was so afraid of losing her.

"What does this mean? I'm so confused," I said to Naomi who was typing a letter on the computer at the reception desk.

"Well, you shouldn't tap the monster awake. If they aren't getting in touch with you, you don't need to get in touch with them, right?"

"Yeah, but that doesn't mean I shouldn't be prepared. I still need to find a lawyer, I still need to raise money for the legal fees. I don't want them taking me by surprise two months from now when I'm not prepared for a battle," I said.

Naomi sighed and then nodded. She fixed her eyes on me sympathetically. "I told you we're going to figure this out. Let's start a media campaign like you said. This whole neighborhood is going to be on your side. We can start rallying the troops right now. Those people might have the judges in their pocket but we'll have witnesses."

I shook my head. I'd strengthened myself to not cry in public over everything, but distress was written all over my face. I'd barely slept the past week. "None of it matters, Naomi. It doesn't matter how many people are on our side if the judges pass a verdict in Ian's favor. Bess will still get taken away from me."

Naomi closed her eyes and it seemed like she was thinking.

"Hey, Iris, can I talk to you?" We had been so engrossed in this conversation that neither of us realized someone had walked up to the reception desk behind us.

I recognized Ian's voice immediately. I whipped around to see him standing there and Naomi jumped out of her chair.

"How fucking dare you!" She squealed and Ian took a step back.

He'd always been afraid of Naomi. He had his hands raised in defense.

"I just want to talk to you, Iris. Just a short and quick conversation. Can we please talk?"

"Naomi, stand down. I'll handle this from here," I said, keeping a firm hand on my friend's shoulder.

Physical violence was not the answer.

"Are you sure about this?" she turned to me with fire in her eyes.

I nodded and then looked at Ian. "What do you want?"

I saw him glance at Naomi nervously and I rolled my eyes.

"Okay, let's step outside," I said.

I didn't want him in even the same building as Bess anymore.

We were standing across from each other and once again it was a cold evening. We were fast approaching winter but I was warm enough, from all the anger and rage that he managed to generate inside me.

"What else have you come to threaten me with?" I asked him.

Ian looked sheepishly over his shoulder and then glanced at me a little confused.

"I'm guessing that is a joke," he said.

That confused me too. "What?"

"What?" He repeated after me and I crossed my brows.

"Look, I know he asked the rest of my family and me to stay away from you, and that is exactly what we have been doing, so you can tell him to call the lawyers off our backs," Ian continued.

"He asked you...what? Who he? What lawyers?"

Ian's eyes grew wide.

"I don't get it. What's the joke?" He asked again.

I hooked my hands on my hips and glared at him. None of it was making sense.

"I just wanted to stop by and personally apologize to you. I hope you know that it was my family that forced me to act that way. I didn't want to get myself involved with Bess and complicate her life. But all that is over now."

The only words that were truly settling in me were that it was over now. Did he really mean what he was saying?

"See, if we knew you were connected to the Dentons in any way, we wouldn't have gotten ourselves involved. I hope you understand. It was never anything personal, Iris."

"The Dentons?" I shrieked.

Ian looked afraid. "Yeah, I mean Silas Denton spoke to me personally. He made himself more than clear. We're backing off, Iris. You won."

My mouth fell open just a few inches.

After a few minutes of me just standing there and staring at Ian in silence and shock, he decided it was time for him to leave.

"Take care of yourself and Bess," he said as he started to back away. "She really is a good kid."

I still couldn't say anything to that because I was at a complete loss of words. Silas Denton? Lawyers? They'd spoken to each other? The Sheffields were backing off?

"Oh my God..." I murmured to myself some time after Ian had completely disappeared from view.

I turned and ran up the steps into the building and found Naomi standing at the reception desk biting her nails.

"What happened?" She asked.

I clamped my hands to my mouth.

"It's over. They're backing off. Bess is going to be fine. I'm going to be fine!" I squealed.

Naomi squealed too and she came running toward me hugging me tightly.

"It was him...it was Silas...he fixed this," I murmured, completely out of breath.

55

SILAS

I was in the boardroom heading up a meeting about the construction project when Lena walked in looking sheepish. She smiled at the others in the room and then glared at me like I'd done something wrong.

"Mr. Denton, Ms. Neilson is here to see you and she says it's important."

My first instinct was to drop everything and go running out of the room to see if she was okay. As far as I knew, based on the numerous emails and text messages I'd received from the Sheffield family—they were backing off Iris.

But I tried to stay calm and not overreact.

"Please take her into my office and let her know I'll be with her shortly," I said to Lena.

I turned to the others in the room and declared that we'd have to speed up the meeting as something personal had come up. Things were progressing well with the project anyway, and there weren't many causes for concern yet. We were on the right track to turn this company completely clean with the help of that project, and I couldn't wait for that to happen.

Once I'd shaken everyone's hand in the room and seen them to the door, I finally stepped out of the boardroom and headed to my office. I hadn't set eyes on Iris in several days and I wasn't sure how my body would react to seeing her again.

Iris stood up from her chair when I walked into the office, and like always, she was like a breath of fresh air.

She was in a casual dress, with thick stockings and a long woolen coat. She looked cozy and beautiful. Her hair was down, her cheeks were still pink from the cold outside, and there was fire in her green eyes. As I shut the door behind me, I realized she might have a bone to pick with me.

"Hello, Iris," I said and she shook her head lightly.

"What made you think you could go behind my back and talk to my ex and hound him with lawyers? I don't remember us having that discussion where I gave you permission to allow you to do that. To poke around in my private matters!"

My eyes drifted over Iris' body and I imagined her naked on my bed again, under me with her legs stretched out. My cock sliding in between those curvaceous juicy thighs.

"Is it over?" I asked her in a deep voice.

I had no other questions for her. I just wanted to know that Bess was out of harm's way and she was doing okay.

Iris glared at me threateningly for a few moments and then slowly nodded. The rage in her eyes was now beginning to turn to something else—relief maybe.

She took a step toward me. "You have got to stop doing this!"

"Doing what?" I asked.

"Playing the hero without asking me first!" Even though she was trying to sound strong, her voice was shaky.

There were a lot of emotions sweeping through her, I could see that. But I wasn't the one drawing close to her, she was the one approaching me this time.

"It's okay to ask for help, Iris," I said.

"I didn't need your help. I had it under control," she replied and came to a stop directly in front of me.

She was close enough to touch. So soft and delicate that she would melt in my arms.

"Okay, I'll apologize then. I'm sorry for interfering. I shouldn't have gone behind your back and contacted my lawyers or the Sheffield family."

Iris looked down at her feet embarrassedly. "You don't need to apologize to me, Silas. You rescued me. I wouldn't have been able to fight them alone. They would have taken Bess away from me eventually."

I wasn't expecting that either. I wasn't expecting Iris to give in.

I reached for her, just softly grazing her arm and she reached up and caught my hand holding it strongly. "I've done everything alone, Silas. Right from when I was a little kid and my parents were using, I was by myself and it's very hard for me to ask for help."

I pulled her into my arms just as I saw a few fat tears roll down her cheeks. "I know you're a fighter, I mean look at everything you've achieved on your own! Look at the kind of work you're doing. You are such a good example for your daughter, but sometimes it's okay to accept help. It doesn't make you a lesser or a weaker person."

She looked up at me, with tears brimming her eyes and she smiled softly. "I don't know how but you always know exactly what to say."

I stroked her soft cheeks with my thumbs, wiping the dampness away. "But I promise, Iris, I will not go behind your back anymore."

"And I promise I won't give you a hard time for offering your help," She chuckled.

I leaned in to kiss her, but before our lips made contact, she pulled away from me with her brows crossed. "What about that girl? The one who walked into your apartment that day? Who is she? She seemed to have a key to your place."

She was beginning to pull away from me when she saw me smile. "That's my baby sister, Sadie. She would love to meet you."

"Then kiss me already!" Iris exclaimed.

I pulled her back in until she fell with a thud on my lips were pressed against hers. Losing myself in her scent and her soft hair and the lusciousness of her body, everything felt just as it should be. Nothing compared to the feeling of being complete when I had Iris in my arms.

56

IRIS

I had my arms wrapped around Silas as we kissed and everything else just seemed to melt away. I finally felt free, like I had nothing to worry about anymore. When I pulled away from him, I felt slightly breathless and giddy.

I smiled at him and he was smiling back at me.

"What are we going to do now?" I asked him.

He reached for my hands, holding them tightly. "Do you have to go to the café?"

I shook my head. "I took the day off. I probably shouldn't have, but I knew I'd need the day off if I was going to come and see you." I said

Everything about him was so perfect. The way he held me, how strong his body was against mine, the way his smile took over his whole face when he looked at me. He was in a sharp suit and tie with cufflinks and a fancy Rolex watch. His hair was pristine and neatly brushed back. He drove a shiny vintage Cadillac, and his face belonged on the cover of a magazine, just like the rest of his chiseled body.

There was nothing ordinary about Silas Denton. I had

never been with a man like him before, but somehow it all felt natural. There was so much more to him than his money, his striking good looks and how magical he was in bed.

"Are we really doing this?" I asked.

He put a hand delicately on my waist. "Do we have a reason not to?"

I was wrong all along. I shouldn't have pushed him away. I should have found a way to make it work with him from the beginning because after Bess, Silas could be the best thing that happened to me.

He had the ability to change my life, and in all the right ways.

"Well, I think there isn't much we don't know about each other anymore," he commented.

I blushed. I didn't think he would still want me the same way, once he found out all my story. "And you still want to be with me?"

He laughed, pulling me to his chest again. "I want you more, Iris. You are real, you are strong and beautiful. You are what I've been looking for all my life. I think I'm falling for you."

His words rang out like music to my ears. I couldn't believe I was really hearing it.

"I think I'm falling for you too," I replied in a whisper. We kissed again, his hands moving over my butt. He squeezed me tightly, pulling me even closer to him. I could feel his cock throbbing and growing between his legs.

I pulled away from him, giggling. "We should talk to Bess first. Do it right this time."

Silas tucked some of my hair behind my ear and nodded. "I'm willing to do whatever you want, my Queen."

We walked up to Bess' school and waited together for her to come out after the bell rang. Silas and I were holding hands and when Bess emerged at the door, I knew she noticed us standing close together. So, she must have sensed there was something different going on.

She'd been asking about her daddy and I figured it would be a good time to break the truth to her, in front of Silas whom she adored.

Bess came running up to us. She hugged me before Silas picked her up in his arms so she could hug him too. She was excited to see him, just like I'd predicted.

We started to walk toward our apartment, while she filled us in on her day and how much fun she was having in school. I cut her short eventually though, because I wanted to get the conversation done with.

"Honey, before we go into the house and get started on making lunch, there is something we need to talk about," I said.

The three of us came to a stop in the middle of the pavement and Silas put her down. She was looking at me and then at Silas.

I reached for her, gently stroking her hair and her cheeks. "I want to tell you the truth about your daddy, honey, because you know we never lie to each other."

She nodded but I could see she was afraid to hear what would come next too.

"He will not be visiting us soon, I'm sorry sweetheart," I said.

Bess' eyes filled with tears immediately. Silas, who was

standing behind her, affectionately put his hands on her head.

"Why not?" She asked in a small quivering voice.

Seeing her cry made me feel like I would burst into tears too.

"He had to go away, baby, I made him go away because he wanted to take you away from me," I replied.

At first, I'd considered lying to her and hiding the truth about her father, but I wanted to keep her safe. I wanted to make sure she got the whole picture. She might be angry for a while, but eventually she would understand.

"He wanted to take me away from you?" she asked, her voice straining.

I kissed both her cheeks.

"But don't worry sweetheart, he's gone now. I told him he couldn't have you because you and I belong together. He will never be able to do that," I said.

Bess wasn't smiling but I could see she looked relieved.

I looked up at Silas for comfort. "And Silas will be spending more time with us, he'll be here to support us and keep us safe. Would you like that?"

Bess nodded and threw her arms around his legs and he lifted her up again.

"C'mon, let's go make you that grilled cheese sandwich," Silas suggested and the three of us walked up to our apartment to spend the rest of the day together.

I couldn't have dreamt up a more perfect day.

57

IRIS

Four months later

It was Sadie's going-away gathering and I knew Silas was annoyed at the idea but she was an adult and capable of making her own decisions. She was on her way to Australia that time.

So, Silas and I had cooked dinner for her at his apartment, and Naomi was invited too, of course. Bess, as always, was the center of attention of it all. She was sitting on Sadie's lap, while Sadie chatted with Naomi about all the places she was going to visit in Australia. Naomi had gone on a vacation there with her family several years before.

Thankfully, Naomi had blended in just fine with Silas once she got to know him, and Sadie and her had hit it off equally well.

Silas danced around me in the kitchen as I prepared to bring the main course to the table, which we had prepared together that evening.

"Careful, it's too hot for your delicate hands," he warned me as I rolled my eyes at him.

I was wearing gloves.

"You're beginning to show your anxiety over Sadie leaving. She's going to be fine. She knows how to look after herself!" I scolded him.

He came over to give me a quick kiss on the cheek as he followed me out to the dining room.

The others cheered as we placed the big dish of seafood paella in the center of the table. It was Sadie's favorite thing to eat and she blew her brother a big kiss.

We all sat down around the table again and Bess was the first to dig in.

"I'd like to make a toast first," Sadie said, tapping her fork against her wine glass.

We smiled at each other and raised our glasses. Bess did it too, raising her glass of grape juice in the air.

Sadie was smiling at us. "I just want to congratulate you both for finding each other, and I especially want to thank Iris for seeing something special in my grumpy older brother who I was sure was going to end up alone all his life."

Naomi giggled, I smiled graciously and Silas leaned in to kiss my cheek.

"And safe travels to you, my love," I declared to Sadie and we all took sips from our glasses.

"Before we start eating, there is something Bess and I would like to talk about tonight," Silas said, standing up from his chair beside me.

"Bess and you?" I looked surprisedly at both of them.

Bess was giggling and blushing, like a girl who'd been hiding something from her mommy. Silas walked over to her and I saw them exchange something quickly under the table. Whatever it was, made Naomi look up at me with her eyes widened and excited.

Silas came around the table to my side again, bending down on one knee in front of me. I saw him popping the velvet box open, but I saw it in slow motion.

"I wanted to do this tonight, before Sadie leaves, so we have the family together. I love you, Iris Neilson, and I love Bess. Nothing in the world would make me happier than to make you my wife."

"Yes!" I squealed and everyone else clapped and cheered.

I fell toward Silas and he caught me in his arms and kissed me. He slipped the ring on my finger, it felt warm and heavy. I hadn't even looked at it properly, I was just too excited at the prospect of getting to spend the rest of my life with the man who made me so happy.

Silas stood up, carrying me up with him. When we finally breathlessly pulled away from the kiss, he turned to Bess. "Come over here you little munchkin!"

I had tears in my eyes and I could see how happy my daughter was. She was old and mature enough to understand exactly what that meant, how it would affect her life and she was very excited about it.

Silas hugged her bringing her up so we could squeeze her together. Then it was Sadie and Naomi's turn. There were happy tears and more hugs. Things had been so stressful and cold for all of us just a few months before, but ever since Silas and I had found each other, things fell right into place.

He gently knocked his head with mine. Knowing it would be like that forever was more than heartwarming.

"I let myself in. I hope I'm not interrupting something." There was a male voice behind us and the room suddenly fell silent.

I turned slowly in Silas' arms to see a handsome young

man standing at the door of the dining room, grinning from ear to ear.

"Alex!" Sadie squealed as she went running to him.

I'd heard of Silas' younger brother just in passing. I didn't really know much about him, except that he was a bit of a maverick.

"I wasn't going to let you leave the country again without saying goodbye," Alex said, hugging his sister.

Then he looked over directly at Silas.

"Looks like you're in the middle of some kind of a celebration here, big brother," he said.

I looked up at my fiancé and he didn't seem too pleased to see his brother.

"It's nice to finally see you again, Alex," Silas replied in a deep firm tone.

I heard Sadie sigh. "Guys, this is my last night in Chicago for I don't know how long...can we just get through it without having another fight? Besides, there is so much to celebrate!"

Silas nodded and smiled. Alex nodded too, but he looked like he still had his guards up. I squeezed Silas' hand and he gently stroked the small of my back.

"I love you, Iris, I'm never letting you go," he whispered seductively in my ear, and I knew he was glad to have me in his arms in that moment.

Nothing else mattered.

The End

∽

Want to meet the next brother of the Denton family? Check

out my next book, **Wanting Secret Baby.** Alex is a hot bad boy who never expected to fall in love so fast so hard.
Read Wanting Secret Baby here!

BONUS EPILOGUE

Thank you so much for reading my romances. I'm an avid reader who lives her dream of becoming an indie author. I enjoy writing about gorgeous billionaires that love to protect their sexy women.
I hope you love my books as much as I do!

Get Bonus Epilogue!

https://dl.bookfunnel.com/cbh7ishgzb

facebook.com/SuzanneHartRomance

amazon.com/author/suzannehart

bookbub.com/profile/suzanne-hart

A NOTE FROM THE AUTHOR

Thank you for taking the time to read my book Rescuing Single Mom. I hope you enjoyed reading this story as much as I loved writing it.

If you did, I would truly appreciate you taking some time to leave a quick review for this book. Reviews are very important, and they allow me to keep writing.

Thank you again for your support, I am incredibly grateful.

Thank you very much.

Love,
Suzanne

ALSO BY SUZANNE HART

All books are standalone novels.

Click Here for the whole catalogue on Amazon!

Turning Good Series

Rescuing Single Mom

Wanting Secret Baby

Second Chance Ex-Marine

Unexpected Roommate

∼

Untouched Series

Her First Game: A Billionaire & Virgin Romance

Her First Dance: A Billionaire Fake Fiancé Romance

Her Accidental Wedding: A Billionaire Fake Marriage Romance

Her Rough Hero: A Military Single Dad Romance

Claiming Christmas: A Mountain Man Romance Novella

∼

Irresistible Bosses Series

Bossing the Virgin: A Billionaire Single Dad Romance

Bossing My Friend: A Best Friends To Lovers Romance

Bossing My Dirty Enemy: An enemies to lovers romance

Bossing My Fake Fiancé: A Brothers' Competition Romance

Irresistible Bosses Box Set

Deceiving The Mob

Made in the USA
Monee, IL
24 April 2020